INADMISSIBLE

INADMISSIBLE

Mark Stern

Carroll & Graf Publishers, Inc.
New York

First Carroll & Graf edition June 1994

Carroll & Graf Publishers, Inc.
260 Fifth Avenue
New York, NY 10001

Library of Congress Cataloging-in-Publication Data

Stern, Mark, 1951–
    Inadmissible / Mark Stern.—1st Carroll & Graf ed.
      p.   cm.
    ISBN 0-7867-0057-2 : $19.95 ($26.95 Can.)
    1. Trials (Rape)—Washington (D.C.)—Fiction. 2. Legislators—United States—Fiction. 3. Lawyers—United States—Fiction.
I. Title.
PS3569.T3896I53 1994
813'.54—dc20   94-4672
                                                   CIP

Manufactured in the United States of America

For
my Mother and my Father

INADMISSIBLE

Part 1

Chapter 1

"Brides in the bath." Peter Fallon pushed his fingers through the untidy tangle of his hair. The phrase—shorthand for an esoteric point of evidence law—had echoed obsessively in his head for a week. The night before, he had dreamed of nubile beauties frolicking in a shimmering tiled pool. A protest, no doubt, against his moribund romantic life. Fallon grabbed the miniature basketball nestled on a pile of depositions and lobbed it across the room. The ball swished cleanly through the hoop mounted on the opposite wall.

Felix Wolfson surveyed him critically from the door. "I thought I told you to go home and get some sleep. You haven't done the Senator any good practicing your free throw all night. He's depending on you."

Wolfson glared aggressively through the thick prisms of his glasses. Fallon grinned back. The broad smile transformed his face, chasing away the traces of moody introspection. He had long ago learned how to deal with Felix Wolfson. Despite Fallon's weariness, humor glinted in his gray-green eyes.

"In my office," said Wolfson curtly.

Stopping to retrieve the basketball, Fallon followed the little martinet into the silent corridor. His lean frame towered over the plump figure before him.

In Wolfson's corner office, Sarah Strasser stood before the

1

broad windows, watching dawn break over Dupont Circle. In her pink silk blouse and blue linen skirt, she looked to Fallon like the last rose of summer. Fallon wondered if he had caught a glimpse of her splashing about in that tiled pool.

"Anybody like me to make some coffee?" she said.

Wolfson turned upon her, his goatee thrusting forward. "If you had worked for me before, you would know that I make my own coffee. And since you are in my office, I will make coffee for all of us."

Fallon winced. Why the hell did Wolfson have to be so pointlessly rude? The little man waddled over to the antique table where he stored his coffee paraphernalia. Wolfson reached for the dark Viennese blend that he served clients after a heavy lunch at Jean Louis or Lion d'Or. In a moment, rich restorative scents wafted through the room. Fallon reached for his cup gratefully. Felix was an asshole, but he made the best coffee in town.

Wolfson placed his delicate china cup carefully on a coaster so as not to threaten the varnish of his gleaming desktop. The whole office looked as though Wolfson had pillaged one of the minor antechambers of Versailles, and he presided there with an arrogance that would have done credit to the Sun King himself.

"Twenty-seven hours to trial," he announced. "And what have we done to deserve our client's trust?"

"The real question," Fallon said, "is what have we done to deserve our client? Did you see him on *Nightline?* The sonofabitch looked so smug that any jury in the world would convict him."

"It was a disaster," Wolfson agreed. "But we'll have the Senator on with Dan Rather tonight for damage control. Leave the media to me. The only audience you need to worry about is the jury."

Fallon perched on the edge of his uncomfortable, undersized chair, balancing cup and saucer. What would a District of Columbia jury make of Senator Cicero Deauville, that champion of law and order and family values, now charged with the rape of Andrea Callas, his congressional aide?

As if in response to his thoughts, Wolfson interjected, "I want

Ken Bradley to sit at counsel table with you. A black face may help us with the jury."

Again Fallon winced. Had Wolfson forgotten about Sarah Strasser, only four months out of law school? What would she think of this sort of hard-boiled remark? And she was bound to pass it on to Ken Bradley. The associates' grapevine was legendary.

"I'd want Ken anyway," said Fallon. "He's been living the case for a week. So it will be the three of us. And Deauville."

Wolfson shook his bald head. "Not me. Three lawyers will start to make the jury feel sorry for the poor beleaguered prosecutor sitting up there all by her lonesome." Wolfson stood to refill their cups from the matching china pitcher. "Where the hell is Bradley anyhow?"

"I passed him in the hall as I came in," Sarah said. "He was going to take a quick shower."

Wolfson pounced. "So I take it you finished the last witness outline?"

Sarah hesitated. "No. Not yet."

"My mistake," said Wolfson with mock courtesy. "I assumed you had finished when I realized that you had given yourself the night off."

"I'm sorry," said Sarah. "I've hardly had any sleep all week."

"Well, don't worry your little head," snapped Wolfson venomously. "The rest of us are all bright-eyed and bushy-tailed. Peter didn't go home and change so he could look pretty," Wolfson added scornfully, forgetting his own outburst to Fallon ten minutes earlier.

Sarah flushed. Fallon noticed the cup tremble slightly in her hand. Wolfson, he saw, noticed this, too, and it seemed to give him satisfaction.

Fallon was about to come to Sarah's defense when, to his relief, Ken Bradley arrived to divert Wolfson's spleen.

"Squeaky clean?" Wolfson inquired sarcastically. "I hope you didn't hurry on my account."

But Bradley knew better than to respond. He drew up one of the uncomfortable chairs. Measured against Bradley's formidable physique, the chair looked like doll furniture.

"Coffee?" offered Wolfson grudgingly. Fallon was amused. Wolfson the impeccable host triumphed over Wolfson the petty tyrant.

"Thank you," said Bradley politely, shooting a wry glance at Fallon.

"So where are we?" Wolfson demanded. "What have you got to show for this week?"

Chapter 2

Only a week ago, thought Fallon. Proof, if any were needed, that all time is subjective.

Cicero Deauville had already arrived when Fallon received a peremptory summons to Wolfson's office. In the far corner, Sterling Gray looked on attentively, ready to do Wolfson's bidding. Gray, a junior partner, habitually functioned as Wolfson's dog's-body.

Fallon recognized Deauville immediately. Since the rape charges had surfaced in early spring, the Senator had become a media fixture. Like most of the Washington bar, Fallon had followed pretrial developments with a mixture of voyeuristic and professional interest.

The Senator leaped to his feet, all southern courtesy. Fallon was irrationally irritated by the choirboy good looks. Light-blue eyes smiled earnestly into his own.

"The Senator has just informed me of a most unfortunate development," Wolfson declared, his small eyes gleaming behind the thick lenses. "His present lawyers are not providing satisfaction. He's asked us to take over his defense. I've told him that Arant and Devries will be honored."

Fallon was dumbstruck. He was well acquainted with the Senator's current lawyers—White and Crystal, the elite criminal defense firm. Why the hell would Deauville fire a top-notch outfit on the eve of trial?

If Wolfson harbored any misgivings, he kept them to himself. The opportunity was too alluring. Sterling Gray had already fetched the necessary papers. He held out his Mont Blanc pen for Deauville's use.

"Just one signature right here," Gray explained deferentially.

The ink was barely dry on the handsome retainer when Wolfson matter-of-factly announced that Fallon would take first chair at the trial.

It was Deauville's turn to be dumbstruck. But Wolfson firmly resisted his protests. "When you hire me, Senator, you're paying for my judgment. And my judgment is that Peter Fallon is the best man for this trial. He has a unique way with a jury. No theatrics. It's a matter of instinct. The jury hears Peter Fallon and they trust him. It worked when he was a government prosecutor, and it works now."

Wolfson smiled. "Peter has one great advantage over myself. When the jury sizes him up, they will believe that Peter Fallon cares about Andrea Callas. It's part of the trust factor. The jury will know that Peter Fallon would never defend Cicero Deauville unless he was sure of his innocence. In a rape trial, Senator, that sort of trust can make the difference."

And so the case of the year had dropped into Fallon's lap a week before trial. Judge Caswell had refused a continuance ("Good," gloated Wolfson, "that may be grounds for appeal"), and Fallon had dived headlong into the boxes of files.

He had needed only a few hours to master the critical facts. Andrea Callas had worked on the Senator's staff for three years. Her relations with her boss had been amicable but never intimate. On the evening of April 18, Cicero Deauville had phoned Callas at her Connecticut Avenue apartment about some papers. When Callas explained that she had taken the file home, the Senator offered to pick them up. The doorman at the Parker House was told to expect him.

In her apartment, Callas offered Deauville a drink. Then the conversation turned unpleasant. Callas complained that she had been passed over for promotion. The Senator took his leave on a rancorous note.

And those were the facts. If you believed Senator Cicero Deauville.

On April 20, Andrea Callas presented herself at the office of the United States Attorney with a different version of events. At first it seemed that the U.S. Attorney might not even seek an indictment. The evidence was that flimsy. The President, a personal friend of Deauville, had railed against the persecution of public figures.

It was an ill-judged move that unleashed a firestorm of criticism. The President beat a hasty retreat to neutral ground; the prosecutor was forced to seek an indictment. Which, to the surprise of some, was forthcoming.

As the pretrial jousting continued through the torrid Washington summer, Fallon had assumed that the prosecution's case was hopeless. Until Senator Deauville became his client.

Chapter 3

A week later, with twenty-six hours now remaining till trial, Fallon looked around at the defense team in Wolfson's office. "If it's just a swearing contest between Deauville and Andrea Callas, we have a good chance," said Fallon. "Deauville is no Mike Tyson."

"We've definitely got more to work with than Tyson's lawyers," Ken Bradley agreed.

Wolfson stood up and pointed a fat finger at Sarah Strasser. "You are Andrea Callas in the witness stand."

Fallon saw Sarah tense in her chair. This role-playing was a standard Wolfson trick. Wolfson moved forward with obvious relish.

"Ms. Callas, what were you doing at eight o'clock on April 18?"

"I was in my apartment reading when the phone rang."

"And who was calling?"

"Senator Deauville. He said he needed to talk to me because he was in the middle of a spiritual crisis."

"A spiritual crisis?" Wolfson's voice was heavy with sarcasm. "Did you believe him?"

"I was a little skeptical. But the Senator sounded very troubled."

"Now Ms. Callas," said Wolfson loftily, "why would the Senator turn to you in a spiritual crisis?"

"We had been lovers for several months until around Christmastime. It seemed natural that he might turn to me."

"So what happened when he arrived at your apartment?"

"He was very agitated. Twice he broke into fits of shaking. I was frightened."

Fallon observed that Sarah had succumbed to Wolfson's realism. Unconsciously, she had assumed the fervent tones of the prosecution witness.

"So, Ms. Callas, you took it on yourself to comfort the troubled soul?"

"No. The Senator asked me if I would hold him in my arms till he calmed down. I agreed."

"Is that all you agreed to?"

"He asked me to massage his temples and I did that, too."

"Is *that* all?" thundered Wolfson dramatically.

"He asked me if I would massage his back and I did."

"I suppose," said Wolfson, "that you adjourned to the bedroom at this point?"

"No, the Senator stretched out on the couch."

"And is *that* all you agreed to, Ms. Callas?"

"No," said Sarah, "I mean, yes and no. After I finished the massage, the Senator began to kiss me and I let him."

"So one thing led to another and you made love."

"Absolutely not. I told the Senator to leave. But he dragged me in the bedroom, threw me on the bed and locked the door. Then we wrestled on the bed and the Senator pinned down my arms. He said he was going to have me whether I wanted it or not. And he said if I resisted, he'd see that I never worked in Washington again."

"So then you allowed him to have intercourse," said Wolfson.

"I was afraid not to."

"Physically afraid?"

"Physically, and afraid of the revenge he might take later."

"Did you think the Senator would let you go if you didn't give in?"

"Absolutely not."

Silence followed this performance. Bradley pantomimed applause. "Her story has problems," he commented. "But Andrea

Callas comes across as an honest young woman from small-town Louisiana."

Fallon stood and slowly paced the Oriental carpet. It was a relief to be out of the spindly chair. "I think there are several points where I can create reasonable doubt."

Bradley said, "I still believe that the prosecution can't show requisite use of force. Callas was basically blackmailed into sleeping with Deauville. That's not rape."

Sarah spoke up. "I researched that one to death. District of Columbia law is very bad for us. If the jury believes Callas, that line won't work."

"Especially not with Judge Caswell presiding," said Fallon. "He's an old friend of mine and he's no Neanderthal. Still, I'd feel a lot better about our case if it weren't for two problems."

Fallon raised one finger. "First, Deauville is lying when he denies he had an affair with Andrea Callas." He surveyed the intent faces of the Senator's defense team. "That's the easy problem."

Fallon raised two fingers. "Problem two is a tough one. And it's called Irene Shaughnessy. Ms. Shaughnessy, it seems, is ready to testify about her own evening with Cicero Deauville in 1990. And that night reads like a rough draft of the Andrea Callas script. Right down to the senator's spiritual crisis, the shaking fits, the whole deal."

Wolfson pressed his pudgy fingers together in a blunt pyramid. "Will her testimony be fatal?"

"If Irene Shaughnessy testifies," Fallon replied, "our client is dead meat. So you might say his fate hangs on the rules of evidence."

Chapter 4

In the moment of silence that followed this summation, Sarah Strasser felt the tension well up inside her again. Thank God she had made it through the role-playing. But now Wolfson would be frustrated by Fallon's doubts. Confronted with obstacles to success, Wolfson's typical reaction was that of a two-year-old—an instant temper tantrum.

Sure enough, Wolfson turned on Ken Bradley. "After a full week, this is all you have for me—an evidentiary conundrum?"

That was typical, too, thought Sarah. Wolfson didn't have the nerve to pick on Fallon. So he just lashed out at the nearest associate.

But Bradley smiled, ignoring Wolfson's hostility.

"You have to admit," said Bradley, "that as conundrums go, it's a pretty good one. The general rule of evidence—"

"Don't lecture me," Wolfson snapped. "We all know the rules of evidence. You'll just have to find a way to keep the testimony out."

They were dismissed. Sarah and Bradley left the office while Fallon stayed behind to talk strategy with Wolfson. The corridors of Arant and Devries were slowly coming to life.

"Join me for a bite of breakfast?" asked Bradley cheerfully, apparently oblivious to Wolfson's last jab.

Sarah shook her head. "Never eat it."

"You're too skinny. When life resumes, we'll invite you to dinner and fatten you up."

Bradley disappeared down the hall. Sarah decided to take the stairs to her own fifth-floor office. As she reached the stairwell, the elevator doors slid open silently. St. John Devries, the firm's patriarch and grandson of its founder, rolled out in his wheelchair. As usual, he looked through Sarah as if she didn't exist. Behind him followed the slim figure of Charlotte Devries, glamorous even in her plain yellow frock. Since St. John's accident, Charlotte loyally accompanied her husband to work in the mornings, returning to drive him home at night. She paid Sarah no more heed than her husband.

To look on the bright side, Sarah considered, as she descended the stairs, she was the envy of all her law school classmates. Three months after graduation, she was working with the legendary Felix Wolfson on the most publicized case of the year. Other young associates, saddled with interminable research assignments and pointless document searches, smoldered with envy.

So what did it matter that the great Felix Wolfson was a tinpot dictator? From the first, Sarah had diagnosed him as a sadistic neurotic with primal narcissistic injury. (She had not obtained a doctorate in clinical psychology for nothing.) His flashes of brilliance couldn't compensate for his deliberate and cunning cruelty.

The late-summer sunshine streamed into her office. Sarah spooned some tea leaves from the box of Earl Grey on the credenza. Teapot in hand, she crossed the hall to the nearest kitchenette for some boiling water.

The problem was not Wolfson, much as she loathed him. It was even simpler than that: She simply did not want to defend a rapist. It was obvious that Cicero Deauville had raped Andrea Callas. Reciting the Callas testimony just now, she could feel the ring of truth. Presumably the Senator had fired his lawyers at White and Crystal because they had failed to conceal their own doubts about his innocence. Sarah smiled grimly. Felix Wolfson would never make that mistake.

"Am I intruding on your thoughts?"

Sterling Gray stood at the door.

"You missed the meeting," said Sarah reproachfully.

"Power breakfast at Duke Ziebert's," Gray explained. Then he laughed. "Frankly, I'd do anything to avoid another of those Wolfson head-bashing sessions. So what did I miss?"

Sarah's mood brightened. There was nothing intimidating about Sterling Gray. As Wolfson's aide-de-camp, he seemed as oppressed as any associate. He listened without interruption, his square-cut face gazing at her raptly.

"If I were making book on the trial," Gray commented when she finished, "I'd put my money on Deauville."

"You're mighty cocky this morning."

"You've never seen Peter Fallon at work. Andrea Callas won't sound so convincing when he's finished with her."

"Even Fallon can't work miracles. No jury will believe that both Callas and Irene Shaughnessy are lying their heads off."

Gray shrugged. "Deauville isn't on trial for the rape of Irene Shaughnessy. Her testimony is irrelevant and prejudicial."

"Well, let me tell you something," said Sarah. "There's something called the 'Brides in the Bath' rule."

"Very colorful."

"The paradigm," said Sarah impatiently, "is a defendant on trial for killing his bride. The bride has been discovered dead in her bath. There's no evidence linking the defendant directly to her death. But then it turns out the defendant has been married six times before, with six drowned brides to show for his efforts."

"A hardworking fellow."

"The point," said Sarah patiently, "is that the evidence will be allowed in."

"What if he had used more imagination in getting rid of his brides and varied his technique?"

Sarah shrugged. "Tougher case. In theory, the evidence is admissible only because of the identical *modus operandi*, the signature touch." It was satisfying to parade the fruits of her research. Sarah tried to imagine lecturing Wolfson or Fallon like this.

"Anyway," she said, "that's the beauty of Irene Shaughnessy from the prosecution's point of view. She's not just claiming she was raped. It's point for point the same scenario as Andrea Callas."

Gray glanced at his elegant Movado watch. "Almost nine. Felix will be howling for my blood." He stood up. "I'll be swamped, but maybe we can grab a bite for dinner."

"If Wolfson gives us time off for good behavior."

"I'll use my influence." Gray laughed. "But maybe we can manage dinner anyway."

He smiled. With more than professional good fellowship, thought Sarah as she watched him disappear down the hall.

Chapter 5

Sarah had just decided it was time to step out for a sandwich when she heard the page over the library intercom. She sighed inwardly. This could only be Wolfson's secretary, commanding an immediate appearance. Lunch would be postponed for hours.

But when Sarah reached the eighth-floor corner office, her eyes fixed immediately on the telegenic figure seated on the Empire sofa. Sarah had never met Cicero Deauville. The low man (or woman) on the totem pole rarely sat in at client meetings. In person, the Senator was almost too handsome to be credible—crystal-blue eyes, wavy blond hair. Unconsciously, Sarah straightened to meet the challenge of this extraordinary stranger.

Wolfson was oozing oily charm. "Sarah (had he ever used her first name before?), I'd like you to meet Cicero Deauville. Senator, this is Sarah Strasser, who has been laboring away in the salt mines to make sure we leave no stone unturned." Wolfson chuckled. "If you'll excuse the mixed metaphor."

A warm dry hand enclosed hers briefly. Now that he was standing, Sarah saw that Deauville was shorter than she had imagined. No more than five feet nine, only a couple of inches taller than Sarah herself.

"I'm pleased to meet you. Felix has been singing your praises." Sarah swallowed her disbelief. The Senator's accent was deep

Louisiana, with the hint of a lilt. Sarah waited expectantly, uncertain of the next move.

Wolfson took her by surprise. "I'd like you to take the Senator to lunch. I've booked a table at Vincenzo. Order a bottle of the Frascati Utrello and drink a glass for me."

By the time Sarah had fully absorbed these instructions, she was on 19th Street, leading the Senator across Dupont Circle. Despite her misgivings about this celebrated client, she was giddy with excitement. Three months after graduating from law school, she was taking Senator Cicero Deauville to lunch. If only there were someone to bear witness.

The worst of the summer heat had passed, and the warm sun on her legs was delightful. Sarah felt as though she had been released from a week in prison.

"Felix says you joined the firm just this summer. What law school did you attend?" Deauville's soft voice was almost drowned by the traffic. Sarah realized that she was being derelict in her duties.

"Chicago," she answered.

"I'll bet you were at the top of your class." Deauville smiled. "No need to answer. Felix Wolfson doesn't hire anyone because of their good looks."

Sarah made no reply. She hated this type of condescension veiled as antichauvinism. They had reached the middle of the circle. Deauville made rather a show of handing dollar bills to several panhandlers. *Give the guy a break*, she rebuked herself. *You can't fault him for giving money to the homeless.*

Deauville's sensitive antennae seemed to sense the makings of a poor impression, because he steered the conversation into serious channels, drawing Sarah out on various issues pending before the Supreme Court. Sarah was impressed that a busy politician would be so knowledgeable. She must have conveyed some of her surprise because Deauville laughed and said, "Don't think that politicians spend all of their time fund-raising. You don't want to believe everything you read in the papers."

Was that a hint? wondered Sarah.

The Senator was obviously no stranger at Vincenzo. They were interrupted several times during the meal by well-wishers. Each

time, Deauville would courteously rise to his feet and introduce
Sarah, declaring with gentle emphasis that she was one of his
attorneys. And each time she would sense the appraising gaze
of jaded male eyes.

When the bottle of Frascati was nearly finished, Sarah was
startled by the silver-haired presence of Terrence McDonald
himself hovering at their table. McDonald, the consummate
Washington insider for nearly half a century, appeared frail and
brittle, his craggy good looks surviving only in memory. Deauville
sprang to offer him a chair, but McDonald shook his head.

"I came by to give you my vote of confidence. I know how it
can be." He shook his head sorrowfully. In his last years, Mc-
Donald had seen his own reputation tainted by financial scandals.

"Mac, I can't tell you what it means to have friends like you
come forward." Deauville spoke with apparent emotion. "When
a friend goes out of his way to stand by you in public, that's
something you never forget." He held McDonald's hand in his.
Then the power broker moved slowly away.

"Now that," said Deauville, "is a gentleman of the old school.
They don't make them like that any more." He smiled bitterly.
"Since last April, plenty of my so-called friends have made them-
selves scarce. You'd be surprised how many Georgetown hostesses have lost my phone number."

"It must be very difficult," said Sarah inadequately.

"You're fresh out of law school," said Deauville. "Maybe you
can bring me up to date. When I was at Vanderbilt I learned
that a man was innocent till proven guilty. In this town, you're
guilty before the trial starts. The only issue seems to be whether
high-priced legal talent can get me off anyway. Isn't that about
right?"

Sarah was suddenly ashamed. Of course he was right. Even
his own lawyer had condemned him out of hand. Before she had
even met her client.

Deauville seemed to be reading her thoughts. He patted her
hand gently. "Don't worry about it," he said. "You have to be
prepared to take the bad with the good when you go into public
life." He laughed. "What say we skip the tiramisu and get an

ice-cream cone down the street? The next few days are going to be plenty tough."

Sarah put the extravagant lunch on her firm credit card—a new experience—and they stepped into the bright afternoon.

An oblong piece of steel was thrust into their faces. "Senator. Senator. Are you going to be taking the stand?" It was CNN. The microphone loomed toward them like a gun.

Deauville faced the camera with humility. "I have every confidence in our judicial system and I look forward to having a cloud removed from my life and my name."

He waved away further questions. "You'll have to talk to my lawyer, Miss Strasser."

The microphone thrust forward. "Will you be putting the Senator on the stand, Miss Strasser? Will he be testifying in his own defense?"

The camera watched her silently. Oh, my God, thought Sarah.

Chapter 6

"Poor kid," murmured Fallon, switching off the set. Still, he had to admit that from a PR standpoint, Wolfson's idea had worked well. The American public had seen an attractive young woman express *her* confidence in Cicero Deauville. And they would picture the Senator's legal representative as a determined novice, not a hired gun. Nice work, Felix.

Fallon paced the length of the expansive living room. Through the floor-to-ceiling windows, the lights of the Kennedy Center twinkled in the soft September night. Under pressure from his accountant to acquire a mortgage, Fallon had purchased the top floor of a wrenchingly overpriced townhouse in Foggy Bottom. But no one had forced him to furnish it. As a result, the high-ceilinged rooms with the polished floors looked more like a gym than a bachelor's flat. A gym with a rowing machine, plenty of bookcases, and a single oversized television.

Fallon grabbed a can of Dr Pepper from the gleaming refrigerator that had rarely seen a vegetable or a cut of meat. The pretrial preparation was over. When the gavel sounded tomorrow, his world would compress to a small bright stage. For a few days, he would know the intense thrill of being fully alive.

The buzzer sounded. Fallon snatched up the intercom. A minute later his visitor arrived at the door.

"I thought it was better to meet here," said Fallon. "Avoid the cameras."

"Good thinking," said the Senator. He looked around uncertainly for a place to sit. Fallon swept last Sunday's *Times* off a chair and offered Deauville a drink.

"What's that you're having?" asked the Senator.

"Dr Pepper."

The Senator was nonplussed.

"Maybe you'd like a beer," Fallon suggested. "Or a gin and tonic?"

The Senator accepted a Heineken and for a moment they sat in silence. Fallon couldn't help but admire Deauville's unshakable cool.

"I'll get to the point," Fallon said. "I want you to reconsider something you told me earlier." The Senator met his gaze. "You told me before that you and Andrea Callas were never lovers."

"I told you that many times," said Deauville pleasantly.

Fallon nodded. "Men say a lot of funny things when they're going in front of a jury. They think they know what a jury wants to hear. Then they write a script with their audience in mind." Fallon finished his Dr Pepper. "Politicians have got their own special problems. Whatever they say is so likely to be misconstrued by the voters at home."

Fallon had no idea how Deauville would react. Clients don't like to be called liars. Senators were not likely to be an exception. Deauville might launch into a self-righteous oration. He might even stalk out the door in indignation.

But the Senator just looked around for a table to set down his beer. With a slight smile, he placed the glass on his own picture staring solemnly from the front page of the *Times*.

"Now what difference would it make to you if Andrea and I ever tumbled between the sheets?" The Senator might have been asking Fallon for his pennant picks.

"This trial is going to be tough enough," said Fallon. "We can make it easier if I don't have to sell a bill of goods to the jury. Callas will describe your affair in exquisite detail. Sterling Gray tells me that there will be corroborating witnesses. You may think you were very discreet. But there will be doormen, waiters, taxi drivers, and neighbors ready to make you look like a liar."

Deauville picked up his beer. "I've been expecting this speech all week. Why wait for tonight?"

"Because I've been too busy to play games with my client," said Fallon sharply. "And I won't begin now. Whatever you tell me is the truth as far as I'm concerned. I just want you to understand the consequences."

"And what about the consequences if I confess to sleeping with a staffer? Will you be around to run my reelection campaign?" Deauville stood up and circled the piles of newspapers. "Peter, I know you believe in me. But do you understand exactly what you're asking? My people in Louisiana can be pretty tolerant. But they won't be happy if they believe they're paying for a love nest in my office."

Fallon rose and stuck out his hand. "Like I said. Whatever you tell me is the truth. You can let me know in the morning."

Deauville's mouth opened, then shut. "You're a straight shooter, Peter. I appreciate that."

"I'll pick you up at eight-thirty."

Watching from the window, Fallon watched Deauville hail a cab. Where the hell was he off to now? The Senator's apartment at the Watergate was only a ten-minute walk away. Even a politician could handle that much exercise.

Fallon put the empty glasses in the sink. In the old days, as a prosecutor, he had been secure in the knowledge that all defendants were guilty. The only question was whether he could prove his case.

Defense lawyers were not well advised to dwell on the guilt or innocence of their clients. Fallon began to compose his closing argument to the jury. With a little luck, the intervening trial would fall into place.

Chapter 7

Sarah Strasser was grateful that the D.C. courts had enough sense to bar the TV crews from the courtroom. If Peter Fallon was going to fall flat on his face, it was best that he do it off camera.

Fallon had sat passively throughout the direct examination of Andrea Callas, apparently fascinated by the prosecution's case. Sarah waited in vain for a flurry of objections. Hearsay, relevance. She could barely restrain herself from running up to counsel table. But Fallon's expression never changed.

Fallon's performance could be inspiring only to Ingrid Torval, the government prosecutor. To Sarah's surprise, Torval looked to be no more than thirty. Her light-brown hair was close-cropped, her face narrow and humorless. At the outset, Torval was shaky, as if she had memorized a script and was terrified of forgetting her lines. With each question, she would look apprehensively at Fallon.

But as Fallon remained silent, Ingrid Torval's confidence grew. In the witness stand, Andrea Callas never took her eyes off the prosecutor, intent on avoiding contact with Cicero Deauville, who gazed at her sorrowfully from the defense table. From the jury box, nine women and three men stared at the profile of the demure witness, listening intently as her story unfolded.

A soft-spoken brunette in her late twenties, Callas radiated the simplicity of her rural Louisiana upbringing. Now that Sarah could see her in the flesh, Fallon's task seemed more difficult than ever. Andrea Callas was obviously the genuine article.

As it became clear that Fallon was giving her free reign, Torval's twangy, insistent voice grew more powerful. With time, she was even feeding Callas leading questions. Finally, Judge Caswell himself admonished Torval to let Andrea Callas tell her own story. Fallon looked on politely.

Torval's direct examination had dragged on into a second day. It seemed to Sarah that they had covered the same ground countless times. If she hadn't known the chronology by heart, Sarah might easily have lost the thread of events. Surely Fallon could have raised some objections to the endless, repetitive questioning.

It was almost noon when Torval finally sat down. When the court recessed for lunch, the defense team pushed its way through the press and piled into a waiting limo on Constitution Avenue. Ten minutes later, the lawyers were ringed around the table of the eighth-floor conference room where trays of food were already waiting.

Fallon loosened his collar and popped open a Dr Pepper. Sarah waited for the recriminations to start.

"Not bad," said Wolfson, spreading a slice of brie on a baguette. "Not bad at all."

"Ingrid Torval is our secret weapon," Bradley agreed. "By the time she was finished, I couldn't remember whether Callas had suggested the visit or whether the Senator had invited himself."

Wolfson wagged a pudgy finger. "The direct of Andrea Callas should have been two hours, maximum. Maybe only an hour. Just a clear simple story from a clear, simple girl."

"And the best part," Bradley added, "is that the jury will remember Ingrid Torval a lot more vividly than Andrea Callas."

Sarah was stunned. So all her hand-wringing had been pure naïveté. Things were apparently going according to plan.

"Are you set, Peter?" Wolfson asked. "Anything you need?"

Fallon opened another Dr Pepper. Sarah noticed that he had barely touched the sandwich on his plate.

"Deauville now remembers that he had an affair with Andrea Callas," Fallon announced. "That should make life easier."

Wolfson laughed. "Well done, Peter."

Fallon pushed a thick lock of hair back from his forehead. His long rangy body seemed ill at ease in dark-gray pinstripes.

"My assessment is just what it was before the trial," he said. "If it's Deauville versus Callas, I'll give you odds. If it's Deauville versus Callas and Shaughnessy, all bets are off."

"Don't be so gloomy," said Sterling Gray, who had remained silent to this point. "Ingrid Torval has no instincts at all."

"Agreed. And she'll screw up her questioning of Shaughnessy just like she screwed up with Callas. But at some point, Torval or no Torval, the jury will start to get a clear message."

"Come on, Peter," said Gray. "You can take Shaughnessy apart even if she gets on the stand. You should be able to paint her as a spoiled brat or an Irish alcoholic."

There was dead silence in the conference room. Sarah looked around, puzzled.

"I'm sorry, Peter," Gray said. "I wasn't thinking."

Fallon grinned. "Hell, my problems with alcohol are no secret to anyone who ever spent an evening with me in the Dubliner in the bad old days."

Gray was obviously relieved to have his faux pas swept aside. Sarah tried to keep her surprise from showing.

Fallon waved the matter away with a dismissive hand. "If Shaughnessy gets on the stand, we'll see what we can do."

"On that subject," said Wolfson, "I'm going to call our private investigator before we return to court. So far he's drawn a blank. We still don't know a damn thing about Shaughnessy except what's on her résumé."

"Who's our P.I.?" Fallon asked, draining his Dr Pepper.

"A guy who works out of New Orleans. He's digging up Shaughnessy's past in Louisiana."

"If he doesn't come up with something soon, it will be too late." Fallon stood up. "I'll go on ahead. I need to talk to Deauville for a few minutes before we start up."

Chapter 8

Twenty minutes into Fallon's cross, Sarah was still waiting for a flash of his much-vaunted brilliance. It was one thing to sit mute at counsel table during Ingrid Torval's performance. But now Fallon was center stage.

Sarah knew, of course, that cases are not won on cross-examination. But surely Fallon would have to puncture Callas's story. Sarah had a series of probing questions ready. Why hadn't Callas's neighbors heard her screams? Why were there no marks of violence? Why had Callas waited two days to come to the prosecutor's office?

These weren't just a lawyer's questions. Now that she was coming to know Deauville, Sarah viewed Callas in a new light. The testimony, which she herself had acted so convincingly in Wolfson's office, now seemed to brim over with problems and inconsistencies.

But Fallon had no intention of asking these tough questions. Sarah could only assume that he was waiting for Andrea Callas to lower her defenses. And, in fact, the witness visibly relaxed as Fallon meandered on in guileless conversational tones.

Sarah glanced at Deauville, leaning forward intently at counsel table. On the stand, Callas was still avoiding the Senator's gaze. She focused on Fallon, readily answering his innocuous questions.

"You've told us," Fallon was saying, "that on April 18 you hadn't seen Senator Deauville socially for three months."

"Yes."

"Was it the Senator's decision to end your relationship?"

"No."

"But it wasn't yours, either?"

"No."

Sarah reflected that Callas had obviously been well coached not to volunteer information on cross.

"So it was more or less mutual?"

Fallon looked at her sympathetically. Unlike Ingrid Torval, he never strayed far from counsel table, maintaining a respectful distance from the witness.

"Breaking up isn't always easy, is it?" said Fallon gently. "Maybe things might have worked out if the Senator had come to you earlier to patch things up?"

"Objection." It was the high-pitched twang of Ingrid Torval. "What Ms. Callas would have done in some hypothetical circumstance is irrelevant."

Fallon ran a hand through his tousled hair. "I'm sorry, Your Honor. I withdraw the question."

Fallon turned back to Callas. "It sounds like you were able to maintain cordial relations with the Senator, despite your problems."

"Cordial? I'd say we were civil. He was my boss."

"But the two of you still had lunch together sometimes."

"We worked together."

Fallon nodded. "Some of these lunches were in pretty nice restaurants downtown."

"You have to do that for business sometimes."

"That's so." Fallon appeared to be searching his mind for a mislaid bit of information. "Were you and the Senator together at the Willard Hotel on April 11?"

Callas flared. "We weren't at a *room* in the hotel. It's a public dining room."

Armor pierced, thought Sarah with satisfaction.

Fallon look surprised. "Of course," he said. "I didn't mean to suggest anything else." He returned to counsel table and ap-

peared to study his notes. From her vantage point directly behind, Sarah could see that he was holding the pages upside down.

"Just one or two more questions and we can let you go.

"On the night of April 18, Senator Deauville came to your
apartment to pick up some papers he needed for work. Whose
photo did you have on your night table that evening?"

Andrea Callas opened her mouth in surprise.

"Objection." Ingrid Torval was on her feet. "May we approach
the bench?"

The courtroom clerk switched on a white noise machine. Its
low roar protected the whispered confrontation before Judge
Caswell.

When the attorneys stepped away, Torval was defiant, Fallon
composed.

"I'm sorry for the interruption," he said. "But let me ask again.
Whose photograph did you have on your night table the evening
that Senator Deauville came to your apartment?"

Andrea Callas broke away from Fallon's gaze. Her eyes shifted
to Cicero Deauville.

"You kept a photograph of Senator Deauville on your night
table, didn't you?" asked Fallon gently.

Callas's voice was barely audible. "I did, but that doesn't
mean—"

"Thank you," said Fallon. "Just one more question. Miss Lucy
Wellington joined the Senator's staff in January. Right after you
and the Senator ended your romance. Is that right?"

Callas nodded.

"When did you learn that Lucy Wellington and Senator Deauville were dating?"

"Objection."

Fallon looked at Judge Caswell with an air of polite
expectation.

"Overruled."

Fallon turned to Callas. "You knew they were dating, didn't
you?" he prodded gently. "It was no secret in your office."

Callas said nothing.

"In fact, the Senator and Miss Wellington became something
of an item in early April, didn't they?"

Callas nodded.

"Thank you," said Fallon. "No more questions."

Ingrid Torval swept forward to begin redirect.

"Counselor," Judge Caswell interrupted, "the Court will recess now."

"But your Honor—"

The gavel sounded. "Court recessed until ten o'clock tomorrow morning."

Fallon looked over his shoulder and caught Sarah's eye. Was it her imagination or had he winked?

Chapter 9

Deauville slammed the door of Wolfson's office. Fallon dropped onto the Empire sofa and unbuttoned his collar. Wolfson stood poised behind his desk.

"Goddamn you, Peter Fallon." Deauville's handsome face was mottled. "I didn't give you permission to destroy my career."

"Let's take it easy, Senator," said Wolfson. "I'll have my secretary get you a drink."

Deauville glared. "I don't want a damn drink. Under pressure from Fallon, I authorized you to admit that I dated Andrea Callas. Who gave him permission to tell the world about Lucy Wellington? You never even had the courtesy to ask me about that relationship."

Deauville strode to the center of the Oriental carpet, scarcely able to contain his rage. "What do you think they're going to say in Louisiana? They'll say Deauville can't keep his cock in his pants, that he hires staffers in order to sleep with them."

"Peter was just doing what he thought was necessary," said Wolfson in calming tones.

Good old Peter, thought Fallon wearily. Just as if he and Wolfson hadn't mapped out every detail of the cross-examination. Fallon slumped back on the couch. He was haunted by the memory of Andrea Callas. The look of pain. What had she wanted to say: "Yes, I loved that man and look how he repaid me?" Just

answer the question, Ms. Callas. This is a trial. We're not here
to talk about the truth.

Deauville was making wild threats to sue for malpractice. Finally, Wolfson had enough. "Senator," he said icily, "you seem
to forget that you are on trial for rape. In comparison to that
crime, your public is likely to forgive your other peccadillos."

He raised a hand to quell a new outburst. The authority in
Wolfson's tone could shut down even Deauville. "Tomorrow
Judge Caswell will rule on the admissibility of the testimony of
Irene Shaughnessy. Your future will depend on that ruling."

Wolfson's eyes gleamed through the thick glasses. "I've just
received a most interesting fax from our investigator in New
Orleans. We need to digest the new information. I suggest that
you leave so that we can prepare your case."

Without waiting for a response, Wolfson escorted him out the
door in the direction of the elevators. Fallon barely opened his
eyes when Wolfson returned.

"I'll make some coffee." Wolfson rummaged among the paraphernalia on the sidetable. "I'm out of Viennese. You'll have to
make do with Barrister's Blend. They make it up specially for
me. I don't offer it to other people—the blend is somewhat
idiosyncratic. A medium roast flavored with spices. Cardamom
for example. Common enough in the Middle East, but a shock
to the American palate."

As far as Fallon was concerned, Wolfson could brew up a cup
of battery acid. He just wanted a momentary respite from Cicero
Deauville and Andrea Callas.

Wolfson respected his silence, busying himself with some papers until the coffee was ready. Wolfson's special blend reminded
Fallon of bitter spiced tea. It also carried quite a kick. In ten
minutes, Fallon was pacing the room, ready to review the investigator's report.

The door opened. St. John Devries rolled across the threshold,
followed by his wife. If no longer precisely youthful, Charlotte
Manning Devries remained for Fallon the embodiment of a
southern belle. And no one, he reflected, could possess wilder
fantasies about southern belles than an Irish kid from
Dorchester.

"Thought I'd look in," St. John declared. "I heard you were very good today, Peter."

"Tomorrow's the critical day," said Fallon. "If you hear I'm good tomorrow, we may have a winner on our hands."

Devries chuckled grimly. "Well, I'll be glad when the case is over. I don't like to see the firm's name associated with this sort of scandal."

Wolfson got to his feet. For God's sake, thought Fallon, this was like waving a red flag in front of a bull. The fights between the two partners, the Virginia aristocrat and the upstart litigator, were notorious.

"This trial will bring the firm more favorable publicity than it's received in years," Wolfson thundered.

"Publicity for what?" Devries shook his distinguished mane of white hair. "Being the firm of choice for rapists? Are you planning to branch out into drug dealers next? That should be a lucrative market."

"This trial will establish us once and for all as the premier litigating firm in town," Wolfson thundered. "Not that litigation is something a corporate boy like yourself would know anything about."

"I know enough to spot big talk when I hear it," Devries sneered. "This case won't establish you as anything if Deauville is convicted."

Charlotte Devries put a restraining hand on her husband's shoulder. To his surprise, Fallon saw her send a beseeching look to Wolfson. More surprisingly still, Wolfson met her eyes and retreated.

"St. John and I are going to stop at Galileo for a plate of pasta," said Charlotte softly. "Would you like to join us? Or is it all work and no play tonight?"

"All work for us, I'm afraid," said Wolfson, the anger gone from his tone.

"Another time," said Fallon.

"Good luck," said Devries gruffly. "Keep me up to date." He wheeled his chair out the door. With a final wave, Charlotte followed.

"Poor woman," declared Wolfson, when she was barely out of earshot. "Married to that fossil."

Chapter 10

"If it isn't the star of the nightly news." Alexis Sobol ushered her ex-husband into the living room.

"I just got home myself," she said. "The meeting ran late. I was showing slides from this summer's dig."

Alexis was still deeply tanned from a summer under the Mediterranean sun, sifting through the ruins of ancient Troy. She was also, in Fallon's considered opinion, too thin. But Alexis always lost weight in the field, then gradually gained it back during the slow months of the academic year.

"I've hardly seen you since you got back," said Fallon. "Did you make much progress on the sanctuary?"

Alexis's dark eyes sparkled. "I've never had so much luck in a single season. One morning I stumbled, well, not literally stumbled, but I chanced on some coins that let us date the east wall to the late Augustan period." She sat back triumphantly.

"I suppose Professor Hauptmann managed to conceal his jealousy."

Alexis laughed. "Barely. It was a wonderful moment. But sometimes, you know, I despair. Schliemann just burrowed through the Greek and Roman levels like a gopher to get to Homeric Troy. It's like following in the wake of a bulldozer."

"Don't be too hard on him. After all, the poor man did discover Troy when no one believed it existed."

"Poor Troy," said Alexis. "How does he put it in the *Aeneid?* *'Lamentabile regnum eruerint Danai.'*"

Fallon laughed. "Please. I'm getting rusty."

Instantly, the pleasant mood changed. "No, I suppose you wouldn't have much time for the classics these days. Or are you planning on sprinkling allusions to the *Rape of the Sabine Women* in your closing argument? It might relieve the atmosphere of unadulterated sleaze."

Alexis sprang up from the couch. "It was bad enough in the days when you were so obsessed with prosecuting criminals that you couldn't remember your daughter's birthday, but at least you were arguably doing something socially useful. Now . . ." She let the accusation hang in the air. "I'll get Molly. She's upstairs doing her homework."

What the hell, thought Fallon, Alexis was always short-tempered when she was hungry. As he recalled it, the Hellenic Society never provided food at their meetings.

All of which, of course, was beside the point. Alexis had married a bright young classics major with a rosy academic future predicted by the best minds at Harvard. She had never forgiven him for turning his back on that ivory-towered life. "Turning your back on *yourself*," she always insisted. Fallon's need for the consuming conflicts of the courtroom remained, for Alexis, an inexplicable character flaw.

"Daddy!"

Molly ran up to him eagerly and Fallon bent to give her a hug.

"I saw you on TV! Outside the courthouse. Mommy wouldn't let me watch, but I saw you at Diane's house."

"Did you see me winking at you? I was winking just in case you happened to watch."

Molly gave him a push. "You were not. You were busy talking. And you looked very serious."

"You saw the wrong part."

"Stop teasing. Listen, everyone at school wants me to ask you. Did he really have sex with the woman? The one who says she raped him."

From the door, Alexis glared at him balefully.

Why didn't she help him? Fallon wondered. He could never

tell what third-graders really knew these days. Fallon tried to imagine himself as an eight-year-old even using the word sex. Between his mother and the nuns, the idea was pretty much unthinkable.

"Listen," said Fallon. "This isn't the sort of thing that's easy for you to understand. Mommy's right. You shouldn't be watching this stuff."

"So what's the answer?" Molly demanded. "What do I tell Diane tomorrow?"

Fallon wracked his brain. "Tell her that the trial is about whether the Senator hurt this woman. And you can tell her in advance from me that the answer is no, he didn't."

"Are you sure? When will everyone else know? When will the judge decide?"

"Later this week. Maybe not till next week."

"Fantastic." Molly was elated by her insider information. "Can I call Diane now and tell her?"

"Certainly not," said Alexis. "You can go finish your homework and you'll see Daddy on the weekend. If he's not too busy with the trial," she added ominously.

"I'll see you on the weekend for sure," said Fallon. "And if you see me on TV, look for the wink."

"You shouldn't make promises that you can't keep," said Alexis as she showed him to the door. "You don't have to deal with her disappointment. I do."

"I'm going to be here," Fallon protested. "No doubt about it."

"Just like Senator Deauville is innocent," said Alexis. "No doubt about it."

"I'm not Senator Deauville," said Fallon.

Something in his tone made Alexis look up. "I know it," she said. She gave him a peck on the cheek. "Good luck anyway."

"I may need that."

Chapter 11

Every time that Sarah replaced the receiver, the phone issued another muted, workplace warble.

The inquiries from the press were dealt with curtly. Sarah simply read the three sentences that Wolfson had scrawled for her and hung up.

But friends, family members, classmates, were not so easily dispatched. Everyone she had ever known had seen her on television these last few days. "No," she said over and over again, "of course, the Senator isn't guilty. Of course, I'm thrilled. Of course, I'm lucky."

Were any of these statements true?

The conversation with her father, the psychoanalyst, was particularly disturbing. He seemed inordinately interested in the amount of time she spent with Deauville and the circumstances of their meetings.

"Dad," she said suddenly, "you're not worried about me, are you?"

"Should I be?"

"What on earth would there be to worry about?"

"I don't know. What do you think?"

It was all she could do to keep from hanging up on him.

When Sarah looked up from her desk, she saw a very thin woman with extremely straight pale blond hair. She was dressed like a lawyer, not a secretary, but hardly looked old enough to have made it through law school.

"I'm Heidi Hollings."

The name struck a chord.

"I joined the firm this week. But you were at the trial when I came by on my floor tour."

Heidi Hollings. Sarah had seen the name on a memo announcing the arrival of the firm's 143rd attorney.

"I saw you on television," said Heidi. "You're even prettier in person."

Sarah was taken aback. Before she could think of a reply, Heidi continued, "How did you manage to land this trial anyway? Everyone tells me I won't see a client or a courtroom for at least a year or two."

Parroting the now-familiar line, Sarah said, "I'm just very lucky. Of course, it's thrilling. I never expected this sort of opportunity so quickly."

Heidi scrutinized her carefully, as if verifying her assertions. *How the hell did she think I got the assignment,* thought Sarah uncomfortably. *By sleeping with Felix Wolfson?* And it occurred to her that, perhaps, this was just what Heidi suspected.

"I heard about Fallon's cross-examination," said Heidi. "Big moment with the photograph on the night table. But I was thinking, how did Fallon know the photograph was on the night table in the first place? Deauville must have told him. And doesn't that establish that Deauville was in the bedroom?"

Sarah was growing increasingly flustered by this total stranger. Just then, Sterling Gray stepped into the office, wearing running shorts and a T-shirt. Sarah observed the powerfully muscled legs.

"I see you've met Heidi," said Gray approvingly. "I thought you could be sort of a big sister to her."

God forbid, thought Sarah.

"Heidi was just worrying about today's cross-examination," Sarah said.

"I understand tomorrow's the big day," Heidi put in.

How the hell did she know all of this? Sarah wondered.

"That's so," said Gray. "Apparently Wolfson finally got some information on Irene Shaughnessy this afternoon."

"Anything good?" asked Sarah eagerly.

"Don't know. Haven't seen the report yet myself. Actually, I just dropped by to see if you had time for a quick bite."

"Can't," said Sarah. "I'm babysitting the Senator."

Gray laughed. "Don't be so blasé. I'll take a rain check."

"I think he likes you," said Heidi when Gray was gone.

Sarah blushed. "Why?"

Heidi shrugged. "Maybe I'm wrong. I'll let you get back to work."

She walked to the door and stopped. "So the whole defense team thinks Deauville is guilty?"

Sarah was startled. "No one said anything of the kind. You think I'm wining and dining a rapist?"

Heidi laughed.

"How old are you anyway?" asked Sarah, now annoyed to the point of rudeness.

"Old enough to drink. Take a break and I'll buy you a glass of wine."

"Thanks," said Sarah. "Another time. I've got to meet the Senator at the Palm."

"I'll walk out with you then. Arant and Devries has extracted its pound of flesh for one day."

It was getting dark outside and the gusty breeze blowing down 19th Street held a hint of fall.

Across the street, Sterling Gray stood at the entrance to the Metro station. Sarah tried to catch his attention, but at that moment he was joined by a rugged-looking young man in khakis.

"Say," said Heidi, "you don't suppose Sterling Gray swings both ways?"

This girl was really intolerable. "I happen to know," said Sarah stiffly, "that Sterling was married and has a child."

"And he also had a very messy divorce. Anyway, I thought he wanted to get dinner?"

"For God's sake," said Sarah, "he's probably run out for a sandwich." She decided to cut the conversation short. "Where are you heading?"

"Home. I live just the other side of the Circle."

"Kalorama?"

"No. 15th and R."

"Are you crazy? That's no address for a single woman. It's dangerous there at night."

"What makes you think I'm a single woman?"

Sarah stumbled. "I . . ."

Heidi laughed. "It's okay. I'm single and I can take care of myself. Believe me. I just finished three years in New Haven." She set off across Dupont Circle, her dress flaring in the wind.

Sarah shook her head. Was she really going to be a "big sister" to this kid? She might have to brush up on the clinical literature. With a smile, she crossed the street to the welcoming oasis of the Palm.

Chapter 12

When Ingrid Torval completed her redirect of Andrea Callas halfway through the morning, Judge Caswell excused the jury. Over howls of outrage from the press, Judge Caswell had decided to clear the courtroom while he considered the admissibility of the next, unnamed, prosecution witness. As the last of the spectators filed through the doors, Sarah took a seat behind Wolfson and Sterling Gray directly behind counsel table.

Ingrid Torval ran true to form. She quoted from a dozen cases to show why Irene Shaughnessy should be allowed to take the stand. The thread of her argument was quickly lost. Judge Caswell removed his glasses, a sure sign that he had lost interest.

But it didn't matter. The rule of evidence was simple. Testimony that showed a consistent *modus operandi*—the defendant's signature touch—was admissible. Irene Shaughnessy would testify about behavior by Deauville that conformed in every respect to the testimony of Andrea Callas. The evidence would come in.

Sarah found the thought intolerable.

Last night at the Palm, she had lingered with Deauville as the crowded room gradually emptied. Maybe they had both had a little too much to drink. Or maybe it was just the dim lighting. In any case, Deauville for the first time dropped his imperturbable mask.

"You've been very good to me these last few days."

Sarah murmured something self-deprecatory.

"Hell," said the Senator, "I know it's been hard watching over me when you'd rather be plotting strategy with the boys."

Sarah smiled. "I hope you don't think that dining with you is work."

"Don't bluff a politician, young lady. I just want you to know that I'll never forget you."

To her amazement, Sarah heard herself saying, "I'll never forget you either."

The Senator's dry hand closed briefly around her own. "Let's hope we're not asked to forget each other." The light-blue eyes smiled into hers.

My God, thought Sarah, shifting on the hard courtroom bench. What was she getting herself into? Was she indulging in some sort of rescue fantasy—maiden saves desperate knight? Or was this just the sort of thing that happened in a high-stakes trial?

Whatever the explanation, she no longer allowed herself doubts about the Senator's innocence. Andrea Callas had seemed credible enough until Fallon's cross-examination. There would be some explanation for Irene Shaughnessy as well. It was up to Peter Fallon to make sure that Deauville would not face the nameless horrors of prison.

"Mr. Fallon," Judge Caswell declared, "I'll hear from the defense now."

Sarah's spine tingled.

As usual, Fallon spoke without notes. Although he maintained his respectful tone, it became clear for the first time during the trial that Fallon and Judge Caswell were on terms of considerable familiarity.

"I'll get right to the point, Your Honor," Fallon said. "I think Ms. Torval has covered all known precedents thoroughly, and I certainly have nothing to add to her erudition."

Judge Caswell permitted himself a small smile.

"Now the situation is this: A United States Senator stands indicted of a most heinous crime. As a result, his name has been dragged through the mud. His personal life has been laid bare for public dissection.

"And what is the evidence to justify this assault on a once-impeccable reputation? The answer is simple—the uncorrobo-rated account of Andrea Callas, the Senator's ex-lover. It is her word and her word only that has placed the Senator where he is today."

Fallon glanced at Ingrid Torval. "What does the prosecution's case amount to? Even now, before the defense has presented a single rebuttal witness, I think the picture for the jury will be clear. Andrea Callas was in love with Senator Deauville. Though their romance had ended three months earlier, the Senator's photograph remained on her night table.

"The Senator did his best to keep on cordial terms with his friend and staffer. But that wasn't enough for her. Not when Andrea Callas learned of Senator Deauville's new relationship with Lucy Wellington. At that point, she was beside herself with jealousy.

"When the Senator came to her apartment on April 18, Andrea Callas made a final attempt to win back his affections. When it became clear that she could not succeed, Andrea Callas decided, in a moment of deep bitterness, to take her revenge. And she came forward with the infamous charges that bring us here today."

The prosecutor was on her feet. "Your Honor, I object to this entire line of irrelevant speculation."

"Sit down, Ms. Torval," Judge Caswell ordered. "This isn't evidence and there's no jury present. Mr. Fallon let you go on for nearly an hour. Please allow him at least a few minutes."

"Thank you, Your Honor." Fallon proceeded as if Torval had never spoken. "Now the court knows, and Ms. Torval knows, that the jury will never convict the Senator on the basis of this evidence. So what does the prosecutor propose? To introduce testimony having nothing whatsoever to do with the night of April 18."

Fallon shook his head. "Ms. Torval knows that our system of justice doesn't permit this kind of evidence. A defendant stands trial only for the crime of which he is accused. Not for crimes with which he's never been charged."

All right, thought Sarah. *We've heard about truth, justice, and the American way. Now for the hard part.*

"The prosecutor," Fallon went on, "would have the Court invoke a narrow exception to this fundamental rule—what we sometimes refer to as the 'Brides in the Bath' exception. But as the prosecutor well knows, this exception permits only evidence of *modus operandi.*"

"But Mr. Fallon," Judge Caswell interrupted. "Isn't that exactly the case here? Miss Shaughnessy isn't simply going to testify about an alleged rape. The witness will describe an identical *modus operandi* to that described by Miss Callas. Miss Shaughnessy alleges that your client invited himself to her apartment in August of 1990. She claims that he feigned a so-called 'spiritual crisis' that manifested itself in an attack of trembling. And she will testify that the Senator used the attack to initiate physical contact that led to forcible rape."

Sarah felt as though she has been dealt a crushing blow. The judge had spoken. Deauville's fate was sealed.

But Fallon seemed to welcome the question. Sarah recalled one of his favorite maxims—as long as you have the judge in a dialogue you still have a chance to change his mind.

"Is this really the signature touch, Your Honor?" Fallon responded. "A man asks a woman to hold him in a moment of crisis. Is that a *modus operandi*?"

"Speaking hypothetically," said Judge Caswell, "supposing the answer is yes. Do you agree that the evidence comes in?"

Sarah bit her lip.

"No, Your Honor, I do not. Before the court bends the rules of evidence," said Fallon, "it must be sure that it has not created an overwhelming danger of unfair prejudice to Senator Deauville."

Fallon glanced again at Ingrid Torval. "Who is this witness whom the prosecution hopes will salvage its case? Miss Shaughnessy moved to Washington from Louisiana in June 1990. She became a clerk-typist on the Senator's staff. The office was happy to hire a citizen from the Senator's home state. So they didn't look very carefully into her background. It was enough that Ms. Shaughnessy could type sixty words a minute and answer the phone.

"This trust was an error, Your Honor. And it has now returned to haunt Cicero Deauville."

Fallon halted. Judge Caswell was hanging on his words. "Only one month earlier, Your Honor, in May 1990, Irene Shaughnessy was released from the Oak Knoll Sanatorium in Magnolia, Louisiana."

Fallon paused again. "Oak Knoll specializes in the treatment of substance abuse."

He stepped back to counsel table and picked up a single folder. "I have here a letter signed by Ms. Shaughnessy's physician at Oak Knoll, Dr. Andrew Bounpane. The letter is dated May 4, 1990. In it, Dr. Bounpane advises Ms. Shaughnessy to reconsider her decision to terminate treatment for alcohol abuse." Fallon handed the letter to Judge Caswell and provided a copy to Ingrid Torval. The prosecutor clutched it warily as if it might explode.

Fallon turned to face the bench. "Irene Shaughnessy proposes to testify about an evening in August 1990. She had spent the first part of 1990 institutionalized for treatment of alcoholism. Just three months earlier, she discharged herself against her doctor's advice. I think I understate the case when I say that the testimony of this witness regarding her evening activities in August 1990 is open to the most serious question."

The courtroom was silent as Judge Caswell read through the letter. At length, he lifted his head and turned his gaze to the prosecutor's table.

"Miss Torval, were you aware of this history? I warn you, if the government possessed this information and concealed it from the court, I will regard your conduct as sanctionable."

Ingrid Torval scrambled to her feet. "Your Honor, I had no knowledge of this."

Judge Caswell shook his head. "Ms. Torval, you are aware that we hold the government to a higher standard of conduct than private counsel. We rely on the government for a full and accurate presentation of the facts. I accept your answer, but I am deeply disappointed." He paused. "Now that you have heard Mr. Fallon's statement, is your position the same?"

"Your Honor, I'd like to request a recess so that we can study this letter and make appropriate inquiries."

"Your request is denied. I will not allow you additional time to investigate your own witness. You've had months to prepare this case."

"In that case, Your Honor," Torval said resolutely, "I can only say that the prosecution's position is unchanged. Mr. Fallon is adept at creating a web of doubts. But the basic fact is clear— two women can tell this jury not only that they were raped by Senator Deauville, but that every material circumstance was identical in each case. Let the jury hear that and decide what happened to Andrea Callas."

For the first time in the trial, Sarah felt a surge of admiration for the prosecutor. Ingrid Torval had been dealt a stunning blow. But she was on her feet and fighting. Whatever her shortcomings, this woman had grit.

"Your Honor," said Fallon quietly, "under our system we do not hand the jury all available evidence and tell it to sort things out. The court must decide what is probative and what is prejudicial. And I repeat that the prosecutor seeks to allow the most prejudicial type of evidence from a witness of the most dubious credibility."

Fallon and Torval stood on their feet before the bench awaiting the ruling.

"We'll recess for ten minutes," Judge Caswell announced. The judge disappeared into his chambers, followed eagerly by his law clerks.

In the silence, Sarah could hear the soft hum of the lighting. She was bursting to talk about Fallon's bombshell. The private investigator had come through in the nick of time. But Felix Wolfson, seated beside her, showed no inclination to speak.

At counsel table, Fallon conferred in undertones with Ken Bradley. Ingrid Torval slumped forward in her seat, head propped in her hand. Senator Cicero Deauville sat motionless, his gaze fixed at some point above the judge's empty chair.

"All rise."

It seemed an eternity until the scraping of chairs subsided and Judge Caswell looked out over a hushed chamber.

For God's sake, thought Sarah. *Just tell us yes or no.*

"This is a close and novel question," Judge Caswell began. "And I will be issuing a written decision that sets out my reasoning fully."

I can't bear it, thought Sarah.

But the judge continued. "However, counsel require my ruling now so that the trial may proceed. So I will now rule that the testimony of Irene Shaughnessy is inadmissible."

For a moment, Fallon and Torval remained frozen before the judge. Then Fallon took his seat. His face betrayed no sign of triumph.

Ingrid Torval remained on her feet. She could not keep the bitterness out of her voice. "The prosecution notes its objection."

"Your objection is noted, Ms. Torval. I will reopen the courtroom now. Please be ready to call your next witness."

Chapter 13

"Is that a Renoir?" Sarah asked Ken Bradley.

A clammy hand fell upon her bare shoulder.

"Max Liebermann. One of the German Impressionists. My grandfather collected them."

"They're lovely." Sarah managed a smile. Wolfson in a dinner jacket reminded her of Toad of Toad Hall. But his magnificent Georgetown home brimmed with remarkable paintings and objets d'art.

"You outshine the paintings in that dress," said Wolfson, his voice dripping treacle.

"I don't often get a chance to put on formal clothes," said Sarah. "I have to seize the occasion."

"And quite an occasion it is." Wolfson filled their glasses from a magnum of Veuve Clicquot. "I see Terry McDonald across the room. He's just come in with Senator Sharpman. I'd better welcome them."

Wolfson scuttled across the room, lighted tonight by hundreds of candles. In the next room, Ridgewell's was setting out an extraordinary spread.

"I like him better when he's bellowing abuse," said Sarah. "At least you know where you stand."

"Oh, you stand fine with Felix Wolfson," said Bradley, "just as long as you don't turn your back."

46

Sarah was surprised. "I thought you had made your peace with him?"

"So did I. Till today. You know what he said to me after the verdict? His exact words: 'Now you see how it's done—maybe next time you can be of some help.'"

"What does that mean?"

"How the hell do I know? But I'm up for partnership in January. And Wolfson is the head of the associate evaluation committee."

Sarah laughed. "They have to make you a partner."

"You mean it would look bad if they canned their only senior black associate?"

Sarah felt her face go hot. "I meant that you're a star."

Bradley smiled grimly. "We'll see."

"Where's your wife?" Sarah asked, looking around.

"Begged off. Truth is, she can't stand Wolfson. Thinks I'm a hypocrite for working with him."

"Sarah!" Heidi Hollings advanced, drink in hand. In her scanty evening dress, her arms and legs were almost painfully thin. For the occasion, she had pulled her pale-blond hair into a bun.

"Sterling saw me rubbernecking at the courtroom and asked me to the party. Congratulations to both of you."

"Thank God it's over," said Bradley. "I'm going to sleep for a week."

"You must be joking," said Heidi. "Your twins are under five."

Bradley laughed. "How'd you know that?"

"She knows everything," said Sarah.

"It took the jury only two and half hours," Heidi went on. "I wonder how long they would have taken if they had heard Irene Shaughnessy?"

"That's one thing we'll never know," said Bradley.

"You all saved the Deauville bacon on that one," pronounced Heidi sagely.

Undoubtedly true, thought Sarah uncomfortably. But there was a reason why the courts didn't admit testimony like Irene Shaughnessy's.

They were interrupted by the ringing tones of a silver fork on crystal. Felix Wolfson was calling for attention. He smiled at the glittering assemblage, candle flames flickering in the prisms of his glasses.

"I had meant to ask one or two of Cicero Deauville's closest friends for a small supper," Wolfson began, "and here you are." The crowd laughed and applauded. "We have all heard too much talk lately. Tonight is for celebration. So I give you, Senator Deauville."

Glasses extended forward in the candlelight. Cicero Deauville, who had been hidden by a knot of well-wishers, stepped out to receive the toast. Sarah's pulse quickened. Deauville in evening clothes was magnificent.

"My friends." The Senator paused. "My *friends*. That's really all I want to say. You are my friends. My friends have stood by me in my darkest moments, never losing faith in me. And I will never forget any of you."

Sarah thought back to her first lunch with the Senator at Vincenzo a week ago (an eternity ago), when Deauville had remarked bitterly on his fair-weather following.

"I can't let this moment go by with saying thank you to my lawyers," said Deauville. "They all have my undying gratitude, especially my old friend Felix Wolfson. But one of my lawyers in particular deserves my special, personal blessing."

Sarah's heart pounded. *My God*, she thought, *he's going to single me out in front of these people.*

"To Peter Fallon," Deauville raised his glass.

Sarah felt a mixture of relief and disappointment as she looked around for Fallon. Following Deauville's gaze, she spotted him leaning against a doorframe, cradling a tumblerful of some dark liquid. He nodded awkwardly as the crowd applauded.

Fallon's dinner jacket was an obvious rental, the tie preknotted. Even the shoes didn't look to be his own. Why didn't Sterling Gray escort Fallon to his own tailor at gunpoint?

As the glitterati surged toward the buffet, Sarah tried to make her way toward Deauville. She had not had a moment alone with him since the courtroom exploded that morning.

But she had to wait her turn as Deauville exchanged handshakes and kisses with political celebrities and Georgetown hostesses. With some difficulty, St. John Devries maneuvered his way through the throng. Deauville promptly sank to one knee for a private chat with the patriarch in the wheelchair. Across the room, Charlotte Devries, breathtaking in a simple black creation, laughed at some witticism of Wolfson's. Their host was certainly in fine form.

"Sarah." Deauville smiled when she finally made her way to his side. "I've been looking for you."

"I've been looking *at* you," she said. "It's not easy to get a chance to talk to you tonight."

"It's wonderful to have so many of my good friends together like this," said Deauville without irony.

"It's not a night for a tête-à-tête," Sarah agreed. "I suppose that will have to wait till the excitement dies down." Would he take the hint? she wondered.

"Tomorrow morning I'm on a plane to Baton Rouge," said Deauville. "There's a lot of damage to be mended. Fortunately, I'm not up for four more years." The Senator caught the eye of a bejeweled buxom figure with close-cropped gray hair. "Margot, how wonderful of you to come."

Sarah waited a moment to see if Deauville would resume their conversation. Then she turned to the heavily laden dinner table that already looked as though it had been ravaged by a pack of wild animals.

"Don't feel bad."

It was Heidi Hollings.

"Who feels bad?" retorted Sarah irritably.

"Politicians are notoriously unreliable. It's nothing personal."

"I don't know what you're talking about."

Heidi shrugged her thin shoulders. "Did you notice that he brought Lucy Wellington?"

Sarah's stomach tightened. "I don't know what she looks like."

"Interesting, but not what you'd call pretty. Like Andrea Callas in that respect."

Sterling Gray approached with a full plate of food. "Seems you two are always together."

"Heidi was just pointing out Lucy Wellington."

"Yes," said Gray, "she's driving the Senator over to *Nightline* later."

"He's on tonight?"

"Wolfson arranged it. A lot of hard political work ahead for the Senator." Gray smiled. "As for us, it's back to the salt mines. No more glamour for the worker bees."

"Does that make Wolfson a queen bee?" Heidi mused.

"Is anything the matter?" Gray asked Sarah. "You look a little out of sorts."

"It's just the excitement."

Chapter 14

Fallon put his feet up on the porch railing. The patent leather of his rented shoes glinted in the streetlight. With the wind picking up, it was almost chilly. He hugged the dinner jacket more closely.

The screen door swung open. Alexis handed him a glass.

"I only keep the Dr Pepper for you. Molly won't touch the stuff."

"Just as well," said Fallon. "It's packed with caffeine."

The cicadas chirped noisily.

"It was nice of you to come by tonight. It meant a lot to Molly. She can brag to all her friends about her dad the TV lawyer."

Fallon laughed. "In the future we will all be famous for fifteen minutes. Is that what Warhol said? I guess I've had my fifteen."

"There will be other cases."

"Well, I hope I feel better about the next one."

Alexis rocked quietly in her chair.

"Nice vest," said Fallon.

"I bought it in Crete this summer. You'll have to see it in the light."

"It was sort of ironic, wasn't it?" said Fallon. "My railing on about Irene Shaughnessy's alcohol problem. The old pot-calling-the-kettle syndrome, don't you think?"

"Don't be silly. You never had to go to a clinic to dry out."

"Maybe I should have," said Fallon.

"You managed to pull yourself together on your own. It took a lot of strength."

Fallon looked through the curtainless windows of the house across the street. A father was crisscrossing the living room with an infant on his shoulder. Fallon could hear the crying through the open windows.

"Do you think it would have made a difference if I had gotten it under control sooner?" he asked. "To us, I mean."

Alexis looked straight ahead. "It's all water under the bridge now. A moot point as you lawyers say."

"You're sure about that?" said Fallon.

"We've gone our separate ways, haven't we? You with your bachelor pad and your women."

Fallon laughed. "That's a knee-slapper." She made no response. He didn't ask Alexis about her men. Even now he wasn't sure he could bear the answer.

"Anyhow," said Alexis, "it's made a difference to Molly. I'd give you fair marks as a father these days."

"Glad to know I do something right," said Fallon.

"Well, you're a hell of a lawyer. If I ever a commit a crime, I'm coming straight to you. It looks like you can get anyone off."

The autumn wind sent a shiver down his spine.

Part 2

Chapter 15

The end of a trial always threw Fallon into a tailspin. So he was ready for the depression that descended upon him in his moment of triumph. For several days he moved listlessly about the firm, perfecting his free throw in his office.

This period of moody lethargy might have dragged on indefinitely. But the West Bank civil fraud case was heating up. The U.S. Attorney's office—his adversary from the Deauville trial—had come to his rescue, scheduling a massive new round of depositions around the country. With a sense of self-indulgence, Fallon chose San Francisco over Wichita. He departed for the West Coast with a contingent of associates and paralegals.

But for some reason, the daily hand-to-hand combat failed to recharge him. His team of hardworking associates seemed bent on proving that they could work longer and harder than even Fallon himself. When Fallon was ready to unwind after a bruising day, the associates were already poring over that afternoon's transcripts. The sole bright spot of the day was his evening phone call to his daughter. Molly, at least, had no interest in the minutiae of accounting gimmickry.

After several days of indecision, Fallon called Felix Wolfson. He was suspicious of his own motives. But it was perfectly true that his team was understaffed.

When Sarah received the summons to Wolfson's office, her

first reaction was horror: Wolfson was pulling her in to work on Forrest Labs. Forrest Labs, Wolfson's largest client, faced a class action on behalf of thousands of women who had contracted cancer by taking its birth control pill. After the emotional roller coaster of a rape trial, Sarah was not ready for Forrest Labs.

Wolfson was on his good behavior. He offered her a cup of Viennese roast. Sarah remembered her own offer to make coffee one morning during the Deauville trial. She was learning.

"I have an assignment for you," said Wolfson.

"I've been doing some research for Sterling Gray—"

"Sterling will be working on Forrest Labs now," said Wolfson.

That seals it, thought Sarah. She had no other line of defense.

"But Peter Fallon called last night. It seems he needs extra staffing for the West Bank depositions. You may be surprised to know he asked for you specifically."

"I'm flattered."

"You should be. Peter's a shrewd judge of talent. You're booked on the 5:30 flight to San Francisco. That should give you enough time to go home and pack a bag. Better make it a big suitcase. The depositions could take weeks."

Sarah swallowed. "My father is supposed to visit this weekend."

Wolfson's eyes blinked in mock horror behind their lenses. "Please tell Daddy we're so sorry."

He picked up the phone. Sarah made her exit.

"I don't know what *you're* complaining about," said Ken Bradley unsympathetically when she charged into his office. "The worst sin that West Bank has committed is good old-fashioned fraud. I'm looking at thousands of cancer victims. Like to change places?"

"At least you don't have to spend weeks on end in San Francisco."

Bradley laughed. "I got news for you, kid. San Francisco is not my idea of Siberia. You're unattached. Go and have a good time."

Sarah was silent.

"You *are* unattached, aren't you?" Bradley teased. "I suppose your heart isn't fluttering for a certain well-known Senator."

"Oh, shut up."

"Drop a card. Address is Ken Bradley, under Felix Wolfson's heel."

Peter Fallon came forward as soon as she stepped into the ornate lobby of the St. Francis. He seemed genuinely happy to see her and, for a moment, Sarah felt more cheerful about the days ahead. After she checked in, Fallon took her to the Top of the Mark.

Fallon, dressed in a heavy fisherman's sweater and jeans, seemed oblivious to the more formal attire around him.

While Sarah sipped white wine, Fallon nursed a Dr Pepper and laid out the background of the case.

"There are plenty of files waiting for you in your room," he added.

"I know," she said grimly. "They were hard to miss."

"Don't worry about them now. By the time we do the summary judgment motion in December, you'll be an expert."

"I doubt it," said Sarah, gazing beyond Fallon at the twinkling lights of the Golden Gate Bridge. "I don't know anything about banking."

"Fortunately," said Fallon, "neither do the bank regulators."

As the days passed, the West Bank drama acquired a human face. Over lunches in Sam's Grill, the cast of defendants became personalities with histories, breathing life into the stack of files in her hotel room.

As junior member of the team, Sarah was not assigned to take any depositions herself. Instead, she functioned as Fallon's ombudsman, sitting by his elbow, taking notes, coordinating the blizzard of paperwork.

Sarah had assumed that the lawyers from Arant and Devries would socialize in the evenings. But the other associates seemed unwilling to take the time. By default, she found herself alone with Fallon.

"My only rule," he said as they settled down to pasta at Kuleto's, "is no business at table."

"Bad for digestion?"

"Bad for the brain." Fallon broke a breadstick in two. "I don't know why you became a lawyer. But take my advice. If you want to stay sane, don't take your work home with you. Even if home happens to be a hotel."

"I've never thought of you as someone who shut the door on work at the end of the day," Sarah replied. "I think of you as the consummate perfectionist."

"Is that supposed to be flattery or insult?"

"Observation."

"Well," said Fallon thoughtfully, "maybe I'm giving you advice that I wish I could take myself: Earn my bread during the day and read philosophy in the evenings."

Fallon grinned at her expression. "Don't look so surprised. What did you think I read in my spare time? *Car and Driver?*"

Sarah blushed. "I didn't necessarily picture you curling up with Hegel."

"I may not have a Ph.D. in psychology," Fallon teased, "but you're talking to a man who wrote a senior thesis on Joyce's influence on Homer."

"Hold on," said Sarah. "You mean Homer's influence on Joyce—the *Odyssey* and *Ulysses.*"

"Wrong way around." Fallon laughed. "It started as a joke in a senior seminar. But my professor was beside himself with excitement. Thought I was dead serious. Launched into a discussion of how we reconstruct and deconstruct Homer in light of Joyce." Fallon shook his head. "He thought I was brilliant. I couldn't let him down."

Sarah laughed. "I don't believe a word of it."

Fallon held up a hand. "I swear. I'll dig the thesis out for you someday."

Fallon adhered rigidly to his rule on dinnertime conversation. In a dozen restaurants, they talked Irish literature, psychology, basketball, and ice hockey. As they traded stories, like eager undergraduates in a coffeehouse, it was difficult to remember that Fallon once seemed remote.

One Saturday morning, Fallon accompanied her to Union Street and looked on while she ransacked the boutiques. "Your wife will look marvelous in this," suggested the sales girl, showing Fallon a short leather skirt.

He laughed. "She's not my wife. And not exactly her taste, I think."

As Sarah returned to the dressing room, it occurred to her that Fallon had gone out of his way to keep their relationship free of sexual tension. She glanced through the curtain to where he sat, wrapped in his fisherman's sweater, absorbed in his magazine. She smiled. Arant and Devries had inflicted Felix Wolfson upon her. But Fallon was more than fair compensation.

By the end of the last deposition, she had "made the case her own," as Fallon put it. If she wasn't yet an expert on banking law, she was certainly an authority on West Bank. She was ready to begin the massive summary judgment motion that would be due just three days before Christmas.

"You never thought you could get all worked up about bank litigation, did you?" said Fallon as they finished their final dinner. The next day Fallon was returning to Washington to spend Thanksgiving with his daughter. She would spend the holiday in New York with her father.

"I admit it," said Sarah.

"You'll see," said Fallon. "It happens in every case. Even when the client is a big corporation and the issues are dry as dust, the fight gets into your blood." He glanced at his watch. "We'd better turn in. Tomorrow will be a long day."

They parted as usual in the lobby of the St. Francis. Sarah wanted to embrace him, but she knew that would only make things awkward. She was saddened, certain that the special intimacy of the past few weeks had come to a close.

Chapter 16

Three weeks seemed like plenty of time for a team of lawyers to turn out a summary judgment motion. Particularly when the weeks included nights and weekends.

But Fallon knew it wouldn't be enough. It never was. The morning of December 21 found him bleary-eyed at his secretary's desk, thumbing through the dictionary.

"What are you doing?" asked Sarah. "Looking for synonyms for embezzlement?"

"Very droll," said Fallon. "I'm trying to look up 'impermissible.' Spell-Check says it isn't a word."

"If Spell-Check says that, then Spell-Check is an ass. Go get a cup of coffee and leave this to me."

Fallon retreated reluctantly to the kitchenette down the hall. He watched with interest as the artificial creamer formed little islands on the oily surface of his coffee.

"That stuff will kill you," said Ken Bradley, grabbing a can of juice from the refrigerator. He yawned. "Well, we've made it through the longest night of the year. Things get brighter from here on in."

"Longest night?" said Fallon. "It seemed long enough to me around three-thirty." Bradley's yawn was contagious. He felt his own eyelids drooping. "What kept *you* here all night?"

"Forrest Labs. I have to go over some deposition outlines with

Wolfson. Lucky me." Bradley glanced at his watch. "We were supposed to start half an hour ago. But he's locked in there with St. John. I think hostilities have erupted at last."

He gestured down the hall at Wolfson's closed door. Over the rhythmic clacking of word-processor keys, Fallon could detect the muffled sound of angry voices.

"Oh, Lord," groaned Fallon. "And they were both on good behavior. It will be hell on all of us if war breaks out."

Wolfson's door flew open. A wheelchair shot out. St. John Devries careened down the hall, his jaw set in anger.

Fallon ran his fingers threw his hair. "For Chrissakes," he muttered, "why can't St. John and Felix kiss and make up?"

A bellow emanated from the corner office. Wolfson was screaming for Fran Rendelman, his long-suffering secretary. "Get Ken Bradley on the phone. He was supposed to be here half an hour ago."

Wolfson stepped out into the corridor, a delicate china cup clutched in his short, fat fingers. His heavy, pale face was sweating as though he had just completed a 10k race. Fallon smiled at the image of Wolfson in T-shirt and shorts. The perspiration on Wolfson's bald head glistened under the fluorescent lights.

"Another 'coffee-break?' " Wolfson snapped at Rendelman as she scampered back to her seat. "If it's not too much trouble, perhaps you could call Lion d'Or and move lunch back to one. And tell the FDA I'll be there at three—if they haven't taken the afternoon off for a Christmas party."

Wolfson spotted Bradley in the door to the kitchenette. "What the hell are you waiting for? I don't have all day." Wolfson nodded briskly at Fallon, then turned on his heel. With a meaningful glance at Fallon, Bradley followed Wolfson inside the office and closed the door.

A minute later, the muffled roar of Wolfson's invective sounded down the corridor like the pounding of a distant surf. Fallon shrugged and looked around for his secretary.

Chapter 17

Sarah Strasser perched on the secretary's desk directly outside Fallon's office. Her long legs swung gently as she perused the sheaf of papers.

As Fallon reached to take the papers from her hands, Sarah rapped him lightly on the knuckles.

"Time's up, Fallon. Time to say goodbye to it."

"I just wanted to check one small thing."

Sarah shook her head. "Didn't I tell you once that you were an obsessive perfectionist? We've got thirty-two exhibits we're attaching to the motion. There are twenty-four lawyers on the service list. This being Christmas week, we've got to get production rolling to make our deadline."

Fallon smiled. Sarah had come a long way quickly.

"I'll be finished in a few minutes," she said. "Why don't you just relax? You must be exhausted."

Fallon was suddenly conscious that he must look particularly strung out this morning.

"Maybe I'll take a quick shower," he suggested.

"Good idea. That will get you out of my way. And when you come back, I'll have the motion ready for your signature.

Fallon grabbed a clean shirt from a desk drawer. He trudged down the corridor, past the stark southwestern landscapes that were this month's visiting exhibit. Could they have picked out anything less evocative of sleighbells, pine trees, and Santas in the chimney? Fallon was getting sick of sagebrush. Walking through the men's room, he opened the door to an adjoining locker and shower area. Beyond, Fallon could hear the ripple of laughter in the weight room.

As he closed his eyes under the hot spray, he imagined Sarah opening the glass door with an urgent question. He chased the intriguing vision from his mind.

Fallon wrapped himself in one of the thick terry-cloth bathrobes neatly stacked beside the showers. Across the room, the door of the sauna edged open. A wooden crutch appeared.

"Let me give you a hand, St. John," Fallon offered.

With considerable effort, Fallon helped Devries to a bench in one of the shower stalls. The contrast between the upper and lower parts of Devries' naked body never failed to startle him. The torso, with it splendid pectorals, was abnormally powerful for a man nearing seventy. In comparison, the withered legs were grotesque, doll-like appendages.

Devries looked on thoughtfully as Fallon proceeded to get dressed. "You filing in West Bank today?"

Fallon nodded. "I'll sign off on the papers as soon as I'm dressed."

"Summary judgment is our last best hope," reflected Devries. "We'll never win if we have to go to trial."

Fallon concentrated on knotting his tie. Since the riding accident, Devries was a changed man. Sarah would probably have a jaw-breaking clinical analysis. In lay terms, the diagnosis was simple: Devries had lost his nerve.

He smiled at the naked figure on the shower bench. "I heard you and Felix having a bit of a spat this morning. What's up?"

Devries waved a hand dismissively. "I had some thoughts about a settlement in the Forrest Labs case. Wolfson didn't agree. But we'll work it out."

Fallon nodded encouragingly. Devries must be going senile. He had been lucky to emerge from Wolfson's office alive. One day, Fallon thought, Wolfson would have enough of Devries' hand-wringing and pull out of the firm altogether.

"You'd better go sign off on those papers," counseled Devries. "You don't want to wait until the last minute."

Fallon was happy to take his advice. As he approached his office, Sarah stepped forward, proffering paper and pen. "Sign on the dotted line."

Fallon appended his name with a flourish. "Let's send this little craft out into the ocean and see how she does."

Sarah began to take her leave.

"Any interest in lunch?" he asked. "We haven't had much time to talk lately."

She shook her head regretfully. "Wolfson asked me to help him out for a few hours. And you know what that means."

With an air of resignation, Sarah walked down the hall to Wolfson's corner office. Depressed, Fallon headed back to the chaos of his office. He should go home and get some sleep. Ready himself for another joyless Washington Christmas party that evening. And tomorrow would bring the dreaded culmination of the merrymaking—the firm's own holiday fete. This year Devries had arranged with some high-placed crony to stage the event at the east wing of the National Gallery.

Fallon had pulled on his heavy tweed coat when the scream brought everything to a sudden stop. A moment later he was racing down the hallway. Inside Wolfson's office, Sarah stood motionless, her hands pressed to her mouth. Her neat pile of papers had dropped onto the Oriental rug. Beside them on the floor, Wolfson's pudgy fingers seemed to be reaching for the new reading matter. The eyes in the jowly face were wide and alert. But Felix Wolfson was unmistakably dead.

Chapter 18

Wolfson's death ruined the afternoon for work and gave the associates fits when they filled out their time sheets. "Professional development" seemed inappropriate. "Intra-office activity" was closer, but not quite on target.

"Of course," observed Ken Bradley, "Wolfson himself would have no problem at all. He'd probably double-bill his own funeral."

Sarah smiled tensely. They were wedged tightly in a small booth in the clamorous basement of the Childe Harolde, a Dupont Circle bistro. While Bradley and Heidi Hollings split a bottle of Beaujolais Nouveau, Sarah ordered a Black Label on the rocks. The cheerful tinkle of ice in the glass was reassuring.

"I wonder who will take Wolfson's corner office?" Heidi speculated. "You think they'll give it to Fallon?"

Bradley laughed. "The body isn't cold and the vultures are already descending on the remains. It's as if Scrooge had kicked off before Marley's visit. No one to mourn his name."

"Oh, I don't know," said Heidi. "Wolfson may have been the biggest bastard around, but he was perfectly decent to me. And the man was absolutely brilliant. Which is more than I can say for St. John Devries and most of the old farts in the partnership."

"He probably just wanted to get you into bed," said Bradley.
Heidi shrugged. "I wouldn't have minded." She laughed.

"Don't spill your scotch, Sarah. Wolfson never laid a finger on me. I'm just saying that there might have been more sides to the man than you give him credit for."

Sarah stared at Heidi incredulously. The girl must feel the need to offer herself to a dominating father figure. Sarah shuddered.

"Talk to us," said Bradley to Sarah. "You're the one with the Psych degree. You know it's a mistake to bottle things up."

"I'm happy to talk," Sarah replied. "There just doesn't seem to be anything to say."

Which was just plain silly. You don't stumble on a dead body every day. Wolfson's face appeared before her suddenly, his eyes alight with anger and accusation as they had been in life.

"I just wish I felt a little grief," said Sarah. "Or not even grief. That would be too much to ask. I just wish I didn't feel relieved."

Heidi laughed. "Half the firm is probably out celebrating. And the other half is wondering whether Wolfson's clients will take a walk." She poured herself another glass of wine. "I suppose it was only poetic justice that Wolfson died of a heart attack. After the Lone Star case, it was obviously the only way to go."

Sarah ordered another Scotch. "Lone Star? I don't think I've heard that one."

Heidi laughed. "Wolfson told me the story himself. I think he thought it would impress me. He was in Dallas doing direct examination of one of his experts."

Ken Bradley interrupted. "It was July and the air conditioning had broken. But Wolfson was on a roll and started frothing the moment the judge mentioned adjournment."

"The result was predictable," Heidi continued. "After two tough hours of grilling by Wolfson, the witness collapsed in the stand. Had to be taken out in a stretcher. It turned out the guy had suffered a severe heart attack. They were lucky to save his life."

Bradley smiled grimly. "But the clincher was this. After the witness collapses, Wolfson comes back to counsel table totally unperturbed. He gestures back at the witness box and says, 'Just wait till you see my cross-examination.' "

Heidi laughed. "The best part was the fiendish little gleam in Wolfson's eyes as he hit the punch line."

"You're making it up," said Sarah.

"I swear it," said Bradley. "Ask Peter Fallon. He was there."

It was already dark when they emerged onto Connecticut Avenue. A raw gust blew across Dupont Circle. With their heads down against the wind, they nearly crashed into Sterling Gray outside Vincenzo.

"Are you guys on your way to drown your sorrows in drink?" inquired Gray ironically. "Or is the pain already subdued?"

"I think we've successfully coped with our grief," said Bradley.

"In that case, I'll join you another time." Gray waved a hand and strode into the wind, a distinguished figure in his sleek Jaeger overcoat.

"Now there's a partner I wouldn't turn down," Heidi observed as she watched Gray cross Dupont Circle back toward the firm. "He's got a weak chin and he's no brighter than he needs to be. But he's got great legs."

Bradley shook his head. "First Felix Wolfson. Now Sterling Gray. You're certainly eclectic."

"Well," said Heidi pertly, "I'm sure there are worse sins than that."

Chapter 19

Fallon sank back in Wolfson's chair and surveyed the dead man's domain.

Wolfson had spent eight or ten hours a day in this chair, the only comfortable seat in his office. He would arrive each morning by seven, long before his fellow partners had even reached for the keys to their BMW's. At night, he would still be burning the oil when they were safely home in Potomac or Spring Valley. On a per hour basis, Wolfson's annual two-million-dollar take was a bargain.

Fallon stood up and walked slowly across the room. A small coffee stain on the Oriental rug marked the spot where Wolfson had fallen. One moment you were sipping your custom blend. The next you were stretched out on the floor. Vanity of vanities.

It was illogical to fear death. That had been a big point with Socrates, though it had never carried much weight with Fallon. Wolfson, on the other hand, was ruthlessly logical. But as it turned out, he never had time to stare into the abyss. Hell, he never even knew that he was going to miss his lunch at Lion D'Or. Way to go, Felix.

Fallon sat in the darkened room, illumined only by the reading light. As the day's tensions drained out of his body, a hundred memories of Wolfson crowded into his mind.

Suddenly he snapped to attention. The light on the desk threw a large shadow across the room. Ken Bradley continued across the office, oblivious to Fallon in the far corner. He pulled at the drawers of the dark walnut cabinet behind the Empire sofa.

"I think it's locked, Ken."

Bradley whirled around.

"What are you doing here?" he blurted angrily.

Fallon was taken aback at the ferocity of his reaction. He tried to smooth matters over. "Didn't mean to surprise you. I was just paying my last respects."

Bradley forced a smile. "You scared the bejesus out of me. I was just looking for one of the Forrest Labs files. The case must go on, Wolfson or no Wolfson."

"I don't think it would be in that cabinet. That was reserved for personal items. Anyway, haven't we set up a special file room for Forrest Labs?"

"It's just Wolfson's own notes on the case I'm looking for," Bradley explained. "But I can find them some other time." He headed for the door. "It's been a long day. And it was a long night before that."

Fallon was inclined to agree. The shortest day of the year had to come to an end sometime. He took a final look around. Someone had rinsed out the Dresden china coffee pitcher. Beside it stood a single vacuum-sealed bag of coffee beans. The Viennese blend that Wolfson always offered visitors. How many times had Fallon sipped the rich brew in this office?

Fallon's eyes narrowed. He searched among the coffee apparatus. Just the one bag of Viennese.

Fallon got on his knees and pulled the wastebasket from under the table.

Fallon rummaged among the contents of the basket, then emptied them on the floor. He frowned.

A shadow fell across the carpet, then withdrew down the hall. "Charlotte?" Fallon called. "Is that you?"

Charlotte Manning Devries reentered the room. Fallon, still on his knees, looked up at the tall figure, wrapped in a fawn cashmere shawl.

"What are you doing on the floor, Peter?"

"Making a mess as usual. How about yourself? If you're look-ing for something on the desk, I might help you find it."

A slight flush crept up under the high cheekbones. In this dim light, Charlotte Devries might still be mistaken for the debutante who had all Charleston at her feet two decades earlier.

"I wasn't looking for anything. I was just sort of—well, Peter, you know how it is. It's hard to deal with death."

Fallon got to his feet. "Do you want me to take you down to St. John's office?"

Charlotte placed a manicured hand lightly on his sleeve. "Peter, that's so kind of you. But I can find my own way down the hall." She kissed him on the cheek and left the room, leaving behind a delicate scent of jasmine.

Fallon plunged his hands deep into his pockets. So Felix Wolf-son was as much sought after in death as he was in life. Fallon switched off the desk lamp, plunging the dead man's chambers into darkness.

Chapter 20

The screech of car brakes on the street below jarred Sarah from her drowsy contentment. She reached her hand out across the bed.

"Any interest in dinner?" she asked.

Sterling Gray rolled quickly on top of her and rested comfortably on his elbows. "Sometimes I believe that food is the only thing that really excites you. Why do we have to go out?"

"Because I'm hungry." Sarah gave him a gentle push. "The male ego will never cease to amaze me. After two hours in bed you feel slighted when my thoughts turn to dinner."

Gray groaned and swung his feet to the floor. "All right. I'm up. Just don't start in with the psychologizing."

Sarah sat up in bed as he walked down the hall to the shower. Sterling Gray, of all people, could use a bit of psychologizing. Of this, at least, she had become certain in the last few weeks as their relationship had suddenly escalated from ironic flirtation.

Gray suffered, thought Sarah, from all the problems of the overbred, New England Wasp, intent on living up to ideals of family grandeur that he had invented in some lonely prep school dorm. (How was that for an instant diagnosis?)

Arant and Devries was not the sort of environment to bolster shaky self-esteem. Unlike St. John Devries or Felix Wolfson, Sterling was no rainmaker. At the same time, he lacked the sheer

legal ability that allowed Fallon to hold his own among the
sharks. Though he drove himself mercilessly, Sterling Gray often
seemed little more than an executive errand boy.

"What are you doing, lying around?" Sterling switched on the
light. "I thought you were starving?"

Sarah shielded her eyes from the glare. "I'll get dressed. You
can decide where we eat."

"That makes sense," Sterling called after her. "I'm not even
hungry."

So what was she doing with this guy anyhow? Sarah wondered
as she gazed at her reflection in the bathroom mirror. Was it
just her infallible knack for picking the wrong man?

"I had an idea," she said as she reentered the bedroom. "Let's
try the new Provençal place around the corner."

"I knew you wouldn't really want me to decide on a restaurant," Sterling pouted.

Sarah kissed him and reached into the closet for a dress.
"Don't be silly. We can go wherever you like."

Sterling shrugged. "I didn't have anything in mind. Let's go
to your French place."

The restaurant was nearly empty. Most of the regular custom-
ers were riding the Christmas party circuit. But Sarah and Sterling had to avoid appearances as a couple. Firm politics dictated
that in-house affairs be kept under wraps.

The waiter fussed over Sterling, elegant in a dark, double-
breasted suit. Heidi might be right that he was no smarter than
he needed to be. And the weak chin was undeniable. But he
certainly cut a dashing figure among the drab legions of Washington attorneys. Sarah thought, with some satisfaction, that they
made a remarkably handsome couple.

"So will you take over Forrest Labs now?" Sarah asked when
they had clinked wineglasses. "You were the number two partner
on the case. You're the logical choice."

"We'll have to see. St. John will make the call."

"I may be missing something," said Sarah, "but you don't
sound too psyched about this."

"Working at Arant and Devries doesn't give you a lot of trial experience," said Sterling. "In ten years in the litigation section, my biggest moment was being third chair at the Lone Star trial."

"Lone Star?" Sarah recalled Ken Bradley's story. "Did Wolfson's witness really have a heart attack on the stand?"

"Sure did," said Gray. "And Wolfson drove him to it. Everyone in the courtroom could see it coming."

Sarah insisted on picking up the check. "It's my turn. Besides," she joked, "if you paid, I'd have to let you spend the night."

"I was planning on it," said Sterling.

Sarah took his hand. "I think I need to be alone. Of course," she added slyly, "you could spend Christmas with me."

"That's not fair. You know I have Jason on Christmas Eve. And then I promised my mother I'd come up to Connecticut Christmas Day. Anyhow, I thought you would spend Christmas with your father in New York."

"He's going out to L.A. to see my brother."

"Will you be okay?"

Sure, thought Sarah, *I love going through the holidays on my own, hoping some friend will invite me along.* But there was no point in making things awkward. "Oh, don't worry about me," she said. "We working girls always manage."

Chapter 21

Tough talk. Worthy of Jean Arthur, Barbara Stanwyck, or some other forties heroine. But it turned out to be a bad night. Letterman wasn't funny. Reading was impossible. Stretched tensely on the bed, bathed in the unhealthy glow of the soundless television, Sarah fought off a barrage of half-named fears.

How old had Wolfson been? Fifty at the most. Only twenty years older than herself. Why did all these men still call her "young lady?" Her thoughts drifted to St. John Devries and Charlotte. Had there been any children? Did they still have sex? She imagined Devries thrown from his horse during a gallop in the Virginia countryside, waking in a hospital to face perpetual consignment to a wheelchair.

Around four, Sarah decided to make herself a cup of tea. At once she fell into a dreamless sleep. When she awoke, the sky was turning gray. Pulling a coat over her nightgown, she stepped out onto the balcony. Ten stories below, the roof deck was bare, the swimming pool covered for winter. Beyond, Georgetown was stirring to life.

The phone rang. The clock on the night table showed seven-thirty. For no reason in particular, Sarah was filled with a foreboding that something had happened to her father.

But it was Fallon, apologetic and mysterious. She agreed to meet for breakfast at Kramerbooks.

When Sarah walked into the restaurant at the rear of the Dupont Circle bookstore, Fallon was already hunched over a cup of coffee, a copy of the *Post* propped open at the Metro section. His tweed coat, draped over the back of his chair, trailed untidily on to the floor.

"You've got circles under your eyes," he said.

"You don't look so great yourself."

He stood to help her with her ankle-length down coat, souvenir of bitter Chicago winters.

"What's up?" she asked. "Do you have a Christmas present for me?"

For once, Fallon was at a loss for words. "I'm sorry—" he stumbled.

Sarah laughed. "Don't look so stricken. I was just joking." She looked around for a waitress. "I'm not at my best this morning. The night was spent in fruitless speculation on the meaning of life. Major mistake."

"They do say that the unexamined life is not worth living. On the other hand, Socrates also observed that no one should engage in serious thought after sundown."

"He didn't."

"He should have."

Sarah sighed. "So what's the occasion for this power breakfast? You've got that preoccupied look in your eyes."

Fallon handed her the *Post*. "Felix made the front page. He would have been pleased."

There was even a picture, Sarah noted, albeit a small one in the lower left corner. Not particularly flattering. But then, Wolfson was no work of art.

"How long had you known Wolfson?" Sarah asked.

Fallon did some mental arithmetic. "He was my boss when I first started at the Justice Department. Say, fifteen years."

"Stop me if I'm being nosy," said Sarah, "but I never quite understood your relationship. Were you friends or just colleagues? The situation was hard to read."

Behind the coffee bar, a waitress put down Mary Gordon's latest and languidly strolled over for their order.

Sarah expected Fallon to seize on the interruption to change the subject. But his next words surprised her. "It goes back to the time of my divorce. Felix had moved on to Arant and Devries, but he got word that I was in a pretty bad way. One day he showed up in my office at the Justice Department. Talked to me like a Dutch uncle. Said I was throwing my career away, drinking like a fish. Which anyone could see. But Felix stuck with it. Fixed me up with a shrink. Offered me a job at Arant, and watched me like an eagle."

The waitress reappeared, silently placing a plate of bacon and eggs in front of Fallon. Sarah received a cup of Earl Grey. She sipped the tea, embarrassed by Fallon's revelations.

"I don't know why Wolfson took such an interest in my welfare," Fallon mused. "Maybe he saw something of himself in me. Though I admit the idea makes me uncomfortable."

Fallon put down his fork. "The point is that I owe Felix a debt. Which is why I got you out of bed this morning. I want you to tell me what you remember about Wolfson's office yesterday."

"What on earth for?"

"Tell me first."

Sarah shrugged. "I remember the body on the floor."

"What else? Where was Wolfson's coffee cup?"

"It was right next to his hand. It looked as though he had been holding the cup when he collapsed."

"Did you see the coffee pot—the china pitcher?"

"It was on the table with the coffee things."

"Ah," said Fallon. "And when you look back, can you remember seeing any bags of coffee on the table with the pitcher? You know, those brownish bags with the Starbucks logos."

Sarah strained to visualize the table. She shook her head. "I only glanced at it for a second. I just can't remember. Now tell me what this is about."

"Probably nothing. I *hope* nothing." Fallon pushed a thick lock of hair back from his forehead. "But I was looking around Wolfson's office last night. And, lo and behold! there wasn't a single open bag of coffee anywhere."

Sarah regarded him blankly. "It must the lack of sleep, but I don't see what you're getting at."

"Well, it's obvious, isn't it?" Fallon countered. "Wolfson died with a cup of coffee in his hand. Ergo, there must be an open bag of coffee in the office."

"Don't say, 'ergo.' It sounds pretentious and doesn't suit you. Anyway, I think I can spot the fallacy. Wolfson presumably had just finished a bag which he threw out."

"It wasn't in his wastebasket. I checked. And the basket hadn't been emptied."

"Maybe Wolfson crossed the hall and threw it out in the kitchenette."

"That seems improbable," said Fallon. "What's more, although there was an unopened bag of Viennese, there wasn't a single bag of Wolfson's Barrister Blend, the one he always drank himself."

"He might have run out."

Fallon gave her an exasperated look. "Wolfson might just have finished the last bag of his personal blend. He might have taken it across the hall to avoid sullying his own wastebasket. But I think it's more likely that someone came into the office and removed an opened bag of Barrister Blend."

"Oh, absolutely," Sarah agreed enthusiastically. "Washington, D.C., coffee-theft capital of the nation. Come on, Peter, why on earth would anyone steal an open bag of coffee from a dead man's office?"

But even as she asked the question, she guessed the answer.

Chapter 22

"Oh, wait a moment," Sarah said. "You can't be serious."

"Why not?"

"Wolfson was fifty pounds overweight, worked like a maniac, never exercised, lived on béarnaise sauce. He was a set-up for a heart attack."

"He used to smoke, too," put in Fallon. "For years. Gauloises blues."

"All right then. But now, if I understand you correctly, you ask me to infer that Wolfson was poisoned. For God's sake, Wolfson was a lawyer, not a Mafia henchman."

Fallon looked surprised. "You think people don't kill lawyers?"

He called for the check, and they shouldered their way through shoppers leafing through stacks of coffee-table books in search of last-minute Christmas presents.

By the time they stepped out onto Connecticut Avenue, Sarah had marshaled her objections. "Look," she said, "I think the idea of anyone killing Wolfson is ridiculous. But set that aside. How would this hypothetical killer get poison into the bag without Wolfson noticing? And why not just put it in Wolfson's cup?"

"You're still tired," said Fallon. "Your brain's not working properly. The poison could have been put in the bag at any time when Wolfson was out of his office."

"That's absurd," Sarah objected. "Your murderer would have

to be a homicidal maniac. How could he know who would end up drinking the coffee? He might kill a dozen people at once."

"He obviously knew better than that," said Fallon. "Wolfson always drank the Barrister Blend himself. He almost never offered it to guests."

"All right," Sarah conceded. "I suppose it was an obvious point. I should have guessed you'd have an answer." She considered the problem. "So what are you going to do with your theory? Present it to the police?"

"No chance," said Fallon. "St. John would have my head. For the time being, this is just between you and me."

They crossed the double lane of traffic into the center of Dupont Circle. Though Fallon's suspicions seemed preposterous, Sarah was flattered by his confidences. "My lips are sealed," she assured him. "But if Wolfson was really poisoned, won't you . . ." She hesitated. "I mean, won't there have to be some tests done on the body?"

"Sure," said Fallon, "I'm having a blood sample analyzed." Fallon dropped some change into the box of a Salvation Army Santa. An image of Cicero Deauville passing out dollar bills to the homeless flashed through her mind.

"It's that easy?" Sarah asked. "You can order a blood sample just like that?"

"Not usually. But in this case there's no family. And it turns out I'm the executor of the estate. Which reminds me, St. John has insisted on a memorial service at the National Cathedral. This afternoon, before the town empties out for the holidays."

"What a scene that will be," murmured Sarah as they entered the lobby of the Devries Building. "I didn't even know Wolfson had a religion."

"Religion doesn't come into it. St. John wants to snare Wolfson's clients and keep them on board."

Sarah got out of the elevator at the fifth floor. It was less than twenty-four hours since she had discovered Wolfson's body. In her mind's eye, the angry eyes looked up at her from the Oriental rug. For a moment she wondered if Fallon's theory were something more than a lonely man's effort to deal with the death of a father figure.

As she headed for her office, she heard the receptionist bitterly complain that the firm Christmas party had been canceled. Just because some partner had croaked on the carpet.

Chapter 23

Ken Bradley was deeply immersed in a sheaf of transcripts. He looked up when Fallon entered the room.

"Hey, man," he said. "Sit down. I wanted to say I'm sorry about last night. I was a little on edge when I ran into you in Wolfson's office."

"I was a little shaken up myself," said Fallon. Bradley looked as though he hadn't slept. But then, Bradley had been working round the clock.

"I can't imagine this place without Wolfson," said Bradley. "What will happen to the Forrest Labs case now that he's gone?"

"I suppose Sterling Gray will take over."

Bradley responded indirectly. "You know the case is headed for trial? Wolfson had ruled out settlement."

Fallon nodded. "St. John was trying to change Wolfson's mind yesterday morning when they were having that screaming fight. I think St. John may inadvertently have triggered Wolfson's heart attack."

Bradley smiled grimly. "Inadvertently?"

"Well," said Fallon, getting up, "I'll see you at the memorial service."

Bradley pulled a wry face. "If we're lucky, St. John will even manage a few crocodile tears."

Fallon returned to his office. As he searched the floor for the basketball, St. John Devries pushed across the threshold. With a powerful arm, he swung the door shut behind him.

Devries was attired for the memorial service in a suit of midnight blue. He dispensed with preliminaries.

"I am aware that my powers as managing partner are circumscribed." Devries smiled grimly. "So I present this proposal as a request. I want you to take over Forrest Labs."

Fallon's heart sank. "I can't do that. It would be slap in the face to Sterling."

Devries shook his distinguished mane. "I've spoken to him. He understands."

"I don't think I can do it, St. John. It's not my sort of case."

"Moral scruples?" Devries inquired ironically. "Problems about defending against cancer claims? I suppose if you could reconcile yourself to defending Cicero Deauville, you can find room in your heart to defend a drug company."

"That's not the problem," Fallon lied. God almighty, what would Alexis say about this? "I've never handled a major products liability suit."

"Don't be ridiculous," said Devries. "Now that Wolfson is dead, you're the only lawyer in the firm who's ever run a major trial. Our litigation department is a bunch of motions men and memo writers." Devries smiled frostily. "Don't be coy. This is the chance of a lifetime. You can take over Forrest Labs and the whole Wolfson stable. In ten years, this could be your firm."

Fallon sat down on the sofa. St. John was laying it on with a trowel. Oddly enough, though, what he said was true. This was the sort of opportunity that Washington lawyers dreamed of as they buckled on their suspenders every morning.

"Normally I would let you drag out this courting process," said Devries, "but I can't afford that luxury. The CEO of Forrest Labs will be coming to the memorial service. It's imperative that he know that you'll be taking over."

Fallon spotted the basketball underneath a chair. Picking it up, he tossed it through the little hoop. "Who am I to stand in the way of a categorical imperative? If my name makes a CEO happy, tell him I'll take over. But I'm not picking up the case till after Christmas. I've got to spend some time with my kid."

Devries flashed a broad, Rooseveltian grin. "Set your own schedule." The hypocrite, thought Fallon. They both knew he would be drowning in Forrest Labs for months.

"By the way," Fallon said, "if you're still so keen on settling the litigation, we might want to have a little chat with the CEO this afternoon. Get an idea of his parameters."

"That would be premature," said Devries airily. "You're in charge now. Run the case as you see fit." Devries continued in his conciliatory mode. "Incidentally, why not bring your daughter out to our place on Christmas Day? Let her ride a pony?"

"Thanks. Another time. I've promised to take her ice-skating."

"Call if your change your mind. We're having a small house party."

Devries wheeled around and headed for the door.

"Ironic, isn't it?" said Fallon. "Yesterday at this time you and Wolfson were fighting over Forrest Labs. Today you're passing the baton to me."

Devries looked around sharply. "We find irony where we look for it." He flung open the door.

That sounded profound, thought Fallon. What the hell did it mean? Still, it was curious that Devries' passion for settlement had evaporated with Wolfson's death.

He retrieved the basketball from the floor. On balance, he decided, Sarah must be right. There had been no murder. And he was in no position to conduct a surreptitious investigation. Years at the Justice Department had taught him that uncovering a murder is hard, dull work. He would follow Devries' advice— take over Forrest Labs, start lunching clients at Jean Louis, become a premier fat cat.

Fallon yawned. It had been another sleepless night. He supposed it wouldn't hurt to take a peek at Wolfson's schedule for the past day or so. Fallon walked down the hall and found Fran Rendelman, Wolfson's secretary. Dressed in unrelieved black, she looked more than ever like a Victorian schoolmarm. It was evident that she had spent most of the last twenty-four hours in tears. Amazing, thought Fallon, remembering the unfeeling arrogance with which Wolfson had treated her.

After they exchanged words of condolence, Fallon ascertained that Wolfson kept his own calendar. Rendelman led him to the desk to retrieve the datebook.

"That's peculiar," she said. "I'm sure it was here yesterday when I tidied up."

"So it was you that cleaned out the pitcher and the cups?" said Fallon.

"Just one cup. That's right."

"You didn't happen to throw away any coffee bags, did you?"

She shook her head. "I wonder where that confounded diary has gone to." She pointed across the room. "And look at that. The latch of the cabinet is broken."

Fallon followed her finger. The door to the walnut cabinet was ever so slightly ajar.

Rendelman blew her nose in a scrap of lace. "No point in having that fixed now. I suppose they'll be taking all his furniture away." Tears welled in her eyes. Fallon put an arm gently around her shoulders. "Come on now, let's get a cup of tea." This was his mother's sovereign remedy for all ills of the spirit.

He looked back at the cabinet and cursed himself for a fool.

Chapter 24

But what had been taken? Having settled Fran Rendelman with a cup of tea, Fallon once more paced the carpet of Wolfson's office. The datebook was gone; that much was easy. But what about the walnut cabinet? Its folders were arranged in tidy stacks. There was no sign of disarray.

To Fallon's surprise, Wolfson had not sent his own files on the Deauville case to storage. Of greater interest was a notebook analyzing the firm's client base. The neatly-penciled notes revealed a well-planned campaign to woo other partners' clients into the Wolfson orbit.

Strong stuff. Devries might not realize it, but Wolfson had all but stolen the firm away. But, intriguing as they might be, these files had obviously not prompted the break-in.

Before leaving, Fallon called building security and ordered that a deadbolt be installed on Wolfson's door immediately. Shutting the barn door on the heels of the herd, he reflected as he pulled on his coat.

In the elevator, he caught himself humming "Get Me to the Church On Time." He wondered what Sarah Strasser would deduce from this Freudian lapse? He was glad he was alone.

He found a cab without trouble, and in minutes he was cutting across the northern edge of Georgetown and into the congestion of Wisconsin Avenue. Suddenly, the incongruous spectacle of a

Gothic cathedral towered above the shops and restaurants. With time to spare, Fallon had the taxi drop him at the edge of the cathedral grounds. He hated everything to do with funerals, and had no intention of spending more time than necessary at the memorial service.

As he strolled among the silent gardens, barren in the December chill, he stopped at the sight of a familiar figure in a double-breasted camel's-hair coat. Fallon had not seen Cicero Deauville since the September victory party at Wolfson's house. His presence at the memorial service was unexpected.

Deauville offered his usual firm handshake. "Peter, I'm glad to see you. I was just trying to collect my thoughts before going inside. Felix's death was quite a shock."

"I would have thought you'd be in Louisiana for Christmas," said Fallon.

"Flying down this evening. I delayed my departure for a day when I heard the news."

"How have things been? Any aftershocks from the trial?"

"Thank heavens, no. If anything, quite the contrary. My constituents see me as a wronged man."

"Yeah," said Fallon, "I figured as much. I saw an item in the *Post* touting you as a presidential possible."

Deauville flashed his telegenic smile. "That's the sort of talk you always hear when there's no election coming up. We'll see what the pundits say two years from now."

Fallon glanced at his watch. Still plenty of time. Deauville looked ready for an extended chat. "We'd better go in," Fallon said reluctantly. "The crowd will be gathering."

Chapter 26

Even in this crypt there was no mistaking them for anything but lawyers. Dark-suited, sharp-eyed, they surveyed the ecclesiastical surroundings warily, mindful of the summary judgment that had been pronounced on their departed colleague.

Perhaps fearing a small turnout, Devries had scheduled the service for a vaulted chamber in the subbasement. The sort of place that, in Europe, might hold the remains of assorted cardinals and princes of the realm.

But Devries had miscalculated. A large crowd thronged into every foot of available space. Wedged between Ken Bradley and Heidi Hollings, Sarah felt suffocated by the wintry smells of mothballs and cough drops.

With some difficulty, Charlotte Devries helped her husband hobble to the front of the room. This dungeon, Sarah reflected, did not offer wheelchair access. An uneasy hush fell over the crowd. Devries, finally seated on one of the uncomfortable folding chairs, began to speak, his full, round tones easily reaching every corner of the crypt.

"We have come together today to pay our final respects to one of our town's greatest legal minds, a gentleman who made us all feel prouder to be attorneys.

"This isn't, in any formal sense, a religious occasion. Felix belonged to no faith. But it is altogether fitting that we should gather in this cathedral to commemorate the passing of a titan of the profession."

Head held at a confident up-tilt, Devries reminded Sarah more than ever of Franklin Roosevelt, only more obviously presidential. Sarah thought she had never seen him so thoroughly in his element as now, presiding over a large, solemn gathering.

Devries had embarked on a series of personal reminiscences. "It was no easy task persuading Felix to join the firm. And for the first few months, there were times when we felt he hadn't quite left the Justice Department behind. I recall one client saying to me, 'St. John, that Wolfson is a bright boy. But he's got to learn he's not enforcing the laws anymore. He's working for me now." Devries paused. "What can I say? Felix was always a fast learner." A ripple of laughter passed through the room.

Sarah gazed at Charlotte Devries standing at her husband's side, hand lightly on his shoulder. What a splendid woman: a classic beauty with those high cheekbones, upturned nose, and wide mouth. The simple black silk dress showed off a full, youthful figure. This wasn't the meretricious appeal of the high-priced face-lift. This was the genuine article.

"And three years ago," Devries was going on, "after I was thrown from my horse, it was Felix who sat by my bed every night to tell me the day's news." Devries stopped, apparently overcome by emotion. "Even when it seemed that I might never leave my bed again, Felix never missed a day. And his support and energy helped me to recover."

Devries slowly moved his gaze across the assembled mourners. "And so, I say goodbye to a friend, a colleague, and an inspiration. Felix Wolfson: *requiescat in pacem.*"

When Devries had concluded, a handful of others struggled to their feet to bear witness. The themes were unvarying: Wolfson's legal acuity, his boundless energy, his contributions to the firm.

Rather to Sarah's surprise, Sterling rose to speak. Sarah noted his appearance with proprietary pride. She felt a flash of annoyance with Heidi Hollings: "a weak chin and no smarter than he needs to be." How long would she let that catty remark bother her?

"Felix and I came to the firm at the same time," Gray was recalling. "Of course, he joined as a famous partner, and I was one of twenty anonymous first-year associates. With my usual luck I spent the next two years working on Felix's cases."

There was a small titter of amusement. Poor chump, thought Sarah.

With understated humor, Gray described Wolfson driving a team of bleary-eyed associates through a series of all-nighters. This was too close to home for Sarah to enjoy.

"The climax," Gray continued, "came one February evening in the middle of trial when a furious blizzard engulfed half the country. I'm sure some of you remember it well—the time that National Airport was closed for three days. Anyway, Felix had sent me to Boston on a wild-goose chase and I found myself snowed in at Logan Airport."

"This one's a killer," Ken Bradley whispered in Sarah's ear.

"I called Felix in Washington," Gray went on. "He was wild with excitement. He had just stumbled on an abstract of the dissertation written by the other side's expert witness. The dissertation was in the library at Syracuse University in upstate New York. I had better get my ass to Syracuse at once and come back with a Xerox."

Gray smiled ruefully. "You can imagine how I felt. I'd had about six hours of sleep in the past three days. All the commercial flights had been canceled. What did Felix expect me to do? Go to Syracuse by dog sled?

"The answer was plain and to the point. Felix didn't care how I got there. But get there I would if I expected to keep my job.

"I won't try and explain how hard it is to charter a plane in a blizzard. Probably only an idiot would have done it. But you're looking at that idiot now. And at eleven o'clock that night, frozen and exhausted, I made my way into the stacks of the Syracuse library."

Gray nodded meaningfully. "You can guess what I found there. Felix Wolfson in a sable coat, feeding nickels into a Xerox machine. He just nodded at me and said, 'Did you bring any change?' "

Sarah joined in the laughter. But at the same time she cringed.

Sterling was no white knight cut from the heroic mold. But there was something so pathetic about this tale. Sarah wondered if she would have had the guts to tell Wolfson to get screwed.

Suddenly, a shrill wail sounded from the far corner of the room, followed by a series of choking gasps. Above the rising murmur of the crowd, Sarah heard cries of "Give her air," and "Let's get her outside." A security guard moved efficiently to the back of the room. A minute later, Fallon came slowly forward, supporting a frail, black-clad woman. Apparently, the occasion had been too much for Fran Rendelman, Wolfson's secretary. Fallon led her slowly out of the crypt.

Sarah was pushed abruptly against the wall as a cordon of attorneys cleared a path for St. John Devries. Mourners, eager to depart, trampled over her coat before she was able to rescue it from the floor. After a struggle, she emerged into the watery December sunshine. A few feet away, Devries was speaking to a clutch of reporters.

Heidi Hollings, enormous sunglasses obscuring half her face, followed her onto the cathedral steps. "What a scene! Half the Cabinet was there."

Overhearing the remark, Charlotte Devries turned from her husband's side. Her delicate face was flushed, but her smile was composed. "My dear," she said kindly, "they all want to make sure he's really dead."

Chapter 26

Charlotte disappeared with the Devries entourage. For once, Heidi Hollings seemed at a loss for words. Sarah couldn't help laughing.

"I think you've met your match—that woman's even more audacious than you are."

Heidi removed her sunglasses. Her eyes were wide. "It's not the audacity that shocks me. But I always thought Charlotte had a thing for Wolfson."

Sarah laughed harder. "Block that imagination before it runs out of control. You may have entertained thoughts of bedding down with Wolfson. But that woman was out of his class."

Before Heidi could reply, Sarah felt a hand on her shoulder. She turned around to find Cicero Deauville.

"I've been looking everywhere for you," he said.

She had forgotten the magnetism of his presence. Was it just the good looks and the aura of power? Or was there something to this man?

"It couldn't have been too difficult to find me. This isn't exactly a hiding place."

"Do you mind if we walk a little?" Deauville asked. "I'd like to talk to you."

Sarah turned to Heidi but discovered that she had vanished. With Deauville at her side, she walked through the cathedral grounds to the quiet side streets of Cleveland Park. She was reminded of a winter afternoon in her senior year of high school. Her boyfriend had confronted her as she was leaving school. He had come to make up a quarrel.

"You probably think I'm a self-centered hypocrite," said Deauville.

"I don't know what you're talking about," she said.

Deauville shook his head. His golden hair blazed in a shaft of sunlight. "I may be egotistical, but I know that there was something between us during the trial. And it wasn't only on my part. Then I disappeared. And you thought I dropped you flat the moment I didn't need you anymore." Deauville stopped. His clear blue eyes looked into her own. "Tell me I'm wrong. But I warn you in advance, I won't believe you."

Sarah laughed. "I knew that politicians were egomaniacs. But you don't really think that I've spent three months pining for you?"

"You haven't answered my question."

"All right," said Sarah. "Let's say you're right and that you're a self-centered bastard. There's no apology called for. You promised nothing and delivered nothing. I don't see that there's anything to say."

It was satisfying to tell a senator to go to hell. Sarah began walking again.

"I didn't come to apologize," said Deauville. "I came to explain, because I want to see you again."

Against her better judgment, Sarah felt a tingle of excitement. But she said nothing.

"I didn't call you after the trial because I wanted to be sure. Sure that I wasn't just reaching out to you in a moment of need." Deauville paused. "I wouldn't have wanted anything like that. It wouldn't have been fair to either of us. So I've waited for time, the great healer."

"Look," said Sarah, "that line might go down well in Louisiana, but I'm not buying. You could have called me once in three and a half months while you were waiting for the great healer to do its work." She felt annoyance mounting inside her. "Let me tell you, Senator Deauville, I have a life of my own. And I don't sit around waiting for you to decide that you're ready to give Sarah Strasser a whirl."

Deauville clapped his gloved hands together softly. "Bravo. But you don't mean a word of that."

"The hell I don't!"

"You know better than that."

"Don't patronize me."

"I've set about this all wrong," said Deauville regretfully. "You're trying to cope with Wolfson's death, and I come blundering in with romance." He smiled. "If all I wanted was a fling with you, you know damn well I would have called you months ago."

They had arrived at a parked limo with congressional tags.

"Let me give you a ride," he said.

"I'll walk."

"Don't be silly. It's cold."

"I don't need a weather report."

Deauville grinned. "Have it your way. But you can't get rid of me this easily. And I don't think you want to."

Deauville climbed into the rear seat. As the car moved off, he rolled down the window.

"Have a merry Christmas."

Sure, thought Sarah. Happy holidays.

Chapter 27

It was nearly dark when Fallon arrived at Wolfson's house. Mrs. Muller, Wolfson's German housekeeper, showed him up to the study. She had been with Wolfson for as long as Fallon could remember. He realized he had not seen her at the memorial service.

Mrs. Muller lingered in the room. Clearly there was business to transact.

"So, Mr. Fallon. How long is it that you will be wanting me to stay on?"

Fallon scratched his head uncertainly. This executor business was going to be a royal pain.

"It will be months before the house is sold. If you could continue to keep an eye on things in the meantime, I'd be grateful."

"My wages will be paid at the same rate?"

"Of course."

Mrs. Muller smiled icily. (Had there ever been a Mr. Muller?) "It is as well to be certain." She took her leave.

Fallon looked slowly around. The room was a showcase rather than a workplace. Operatic memorabilia (Wolfson had indulged a taste for Wagner) were prominently displayed. Some of these looked to be of considerable value. Fallon sighed. He would have to find someone good to auction off the estate.

A PC sat on a side table. Fallon had never seen Wolfson

employ a computer at work. On closer examination, he was not sure that the contraption was a PC after all. At any rate, it was not any kind he had seen before. The keyboard was remarkably simplified, with a lever like a pilot's joystick. This would have to wait for another day.

From his wallet, Fallon drew out the combination to Wolfson's safe. After some fiddling, the door slid open.

Fallon set the contents of the safe on the carpet and began to sort through the small stack. It was a disappointing collection. The usual assortment of documents—passport, birth certificate, house deeds, financial instruments. Each new envelope offered only additional evidence of Wolfson's accumulated wealth. Fallon was on the verge of returning the whole pile to the safe, when he came upon a particularly unpromising envelope without markings.

He bit his lip so hard that a drop of blood fell soundlessly to the floor. The photograph was a black and white eight-by-ten, obviously developed in a home darkroom. As a work of art, its value was negligible.

But the naked woman splayed out on the bed was no artist's model. It was Charlotte Manning Devries. A seductive smile played about the corners of her mouth. The bad lighting made it hard to be sure, but Fallon thought that her hands were tied to the bedposts.

Fallon was filled with a mixture of revulsion and shame, as if he were a prurient schoolboy caught leafing through a dirty magazine. (The nuns would do it to you every time.) So much for his visions of the essential southern belle. Fallon tore his eyes away from the body on the bed.

Holy Christ.

Fallon had been so transfixed by his discovery that he had been unaware of the doorbell ringing. Now he heard voices rising from the stairs. Stuffing the photograph into his coat, he quickly threw the other papers back into the safe. A moment later, Mrs. Muller entered the room.

"Mr. Fallon. There is a gentleman downstairs. He wishes to look through some of Mr. Wolfson's things. I told him you were here."

Sterling Gray appeared behind Mrs. Muller. "Peter. I'm glad you're here."

Fallon nodded his thanks to Mrs. Muller, who turned on her heel and closed the door behind her.

"I should have called you," said Gray. "But I wasn't sure how you would react."

"What's the problem?" Fallon's mind was still reeling from the photograph of Charlotte Devries. He had no clue why Sterling Gray would appear unannounced at Wolfson's house.

Gray opened his briefcase and took out a manila folder. "You know that Felix and I are both on the associate evaluation committee? Felix was in charge of the report on Ken Bradley. He'll be up for the partnership at the February meeting. Last week Felix gave me this." Gray handed over the folder.

Fallon scanned the report quickly. He was aghast. Wolfson condemned Bradley for absence of initiative, client development, ability to think on his feet. Bradley's hard work and intelligence received grudging acknowledgment. But, the report concluded, they weren't enough. It was a blackball.

"How could he do that to Ken?" Fallon asked. "Wolfson sucked the blood out of that man for eight years."

"Want a short answer?"

"If there is one."

"Wolfson was a racist," Gray declared emphatically. "A sexist and a racist. If you look back over his treatment of associates, the pattern is clear."

"I thought he doled out abuse pretty even-handedly," Fallon responded wryly. "What about that story you told this afternoon about Syracuse in the snowstorm?"

"There are degrees of ghastliness."

Fallon was silent. He would not have numbered racism among Wolfson's many sins. But a lot of his notions about Wolfson were obviously going to have to be revised.

"The reason I came," said Gray, "was to look for the original of this report so that no one else would find it. I intend to destroy my own copy as well. There's no reason that Bradley's career should be ruined by this kind of attack. Someone else can write a new report and he'll be judged on his merits."

"Have you searched Wolfson's office?"

"Yesterday. I couldn't find it, though some of the files were locked." Gray looked at him earnestly. "So what do you say, Peter? Am I doing wrong? Or do we give Ken a fighting chance?"

"As far as I'm concerned, the report doesn't exist. Let's see what the next evaluation has to say."

Gray put out a hand. "Thank you, Peter. I was an associate in this firm. I know what hell it can be. Bradley deserves better than this."

He returned the folder to his briefcase. "Are you ready to leave? I can give you a lift."

"Sure," said Fallon. "I've had enough for one day."

Chapter 28

Alexis celebrated the holiday in the European style, on Christmas Eve. Dinner was always the same: a leg of lamb studded with garlic and rosemary. The lighting of the candles on the tree (Alexis would not tolerate electric lights) was a solemn ceremony. But when the moments of wonder had passed, Molly tore eagerly into the heap of presents.

Even on Christmas Eve, Alexis insisted that her daughter be in bed at a reasonable hour. Molly, thought Fallon, was probably the only child of her generation who didn't set her own bedtime and make her parents like it. As the guest, it fell to Fallon to read her a chapter from the Narnia chronicles. Tonight it was Prince Caspian. When Fallon had finished the introduction of Trumpkin the dwarf, he looked down to find Molly sound asleep, exhausted by the excitement of the day. He kissed his daughter goodnight and tiptoed down the stairs.

After the washing up, they returned to the living room, strewn with wrapping paper. "Just leave it," Alexis sighed. "Molly will make a new mess in the morning anyway."

For several minutes he and Alexis watched the flames flicker in the old stone fireplace. In the dancing firelight, her face was burnished a soft gold. Alexis might have been the young student he had first encountered in the stacks of Widener Library twenty years earlier.

This is the woman of my life, thought Fallon. Alexis gazed intently at the dancing fire. Fallon ached to take her hand and pour out his heart. But nothing was simple anymore. There was too much history. 'History is a nightmare from which I am trying to awake.' When Fallon had first come across this declaration in *Ulysses*, he assumed Joyce was talking about the political history of the Irish. As he grew older, he realized he had it wrong: personal history was the inescapable burden.

Alexis's thoughts had taken a different track. "So what have you discovered about Wolfson?" she asked, turning away from the fire.

Fallon had told of her his suspicions. He brought her up to date on his discoveries.

"You don't seem shocked," said Fallon when he had finished.

"About the photograph?"

"The photograph, or Wolfson's hatchet job on Bradley, anything."

Alexis stretched out her legs on the coffee table. "Having known Felix Wolfson, it's hard to be shocked. Though I wouldn't have suspected a fling with Charlotte Devries. Is she still as beautiful as she was in her salad days?"

"Age cannot wither nor custom stale her."

Alexis laughed. "A perfect set-up for Wolfson. The thing fairly oozes with eroticism and power. Assuming that Wolfson distinguished between the two concepts."

"But what would Charlotte see in Wolfson?" mused Fallon.

"I hate to be crude," said Alexis, "but it's been some time since St. John's accident. And Charlotte always seemed to me like a very highly sexed woman."

"I always thought of her as southern belle."

"Are you suggesting that there's a difference?"

"Point taken," said Fallon. "But why Wolfson? No Hercules he."

"Don't be so dismissive," said Alexis. "Women aren't like men. They act on attractions that aren't purely physical."

Fallon felt a pang of jealousy. What man might she have in mind?

"Anyway," Alexis went on, "Charlotte clearly gravitates to

money and power. Why else would she have married St. John? The question is, was Charlotte Helen of Troy, borne away by Paris/Wolfson? In that case, St. John might be a sort of latter-day Menelaus, killing Wolfson to retrieve his bride." She paused. "Or was Charlotte some sort of Medea, killing Wolfson in an act of jealousy or rage?"

"It's nice how there's a myth to suit every occasion," said Fallon. "I suppose either Charlotte or St. John would be capable of murder if they had a good enough reason."

"St. John had all the reason in the world," Alexis replied. "Wolfson stole his wife and nearly stole his firm. Reasonable men murder for less."

"Or Wolfson might have been blackmailing Charlotte," Fallon reflected. "She might have been searching for the photograph when she came to his office the night of the murder."

"What about Ken Bradley? You're not absolving him just because he's a friend?"

Fallon frowned. "I wish I could. But what if Wolfson had shown him the partnership report? Eight years of his life down the drain. Bradley takes his revenge. Then he steals the report from the cabinet. Which saves his career and destroys the evidence of motive. Only he doesn't know that Wolfson had given a copy to Sterling Gray."

"So what next?" Alexis asked. "You seem to be getting sucked into the mystery in spite of yourself."

"Tomorrow I go out to Waverly Hill. I'll take the photograph with me."

"Aha!" exclaimed Alexis. "So that's the reason for the change in plans. Molly gets a pony ride at the Devries estate instead of ice-skating on the mall."

Fallon smiled. "Molly says ice-skating is passé."

"Make sure someone keeps an eye on her," Alexis cautioned. "Remember what happened to St. John."

"Don't worry," said Fallon. "Molly's not going on any foxhunts."

Alexis stood up to make a pot of coffee. Fallon followed her back into the kitchen.

"I'm making the Greek semi-sweet," she said.

"That's fine."

"I hope it keeps you awake. I worry about you when you drive home late on that motorbike. Why don't you get a car like most adults?"

"You used to like the bike," Fallon teased.

"I still do. I just worry."

Fallon took a deep breath. "I don't have to go home, you know."

Alexis looked up from the coffee.

"I don't think that would be a good idea."

"Why not?" He steeled himself. "Is there someone else?"

She shook her head. "It's not that. You know I'll always love you. But there's a time . . ." She looked at him helplessly. "There's a time. And when it passes, you can't get it back. You're the one who used to quote Heraclites; how you can't put your feet in the same river twice."

"I don't want to relive the past. I want a future."

Fallon stood still in the middle of the kitchen. Alexis was about to step into his arms. But she turned away. "It's been a lovely evening. Let's not spoil it."

There were so many things to say. But love was not like law. You didn't win by pleading your case.

"Okay," said Fallon. "Let's have coffee."

Chapter 29

The weather on Christmas Day played one of its typical Washington tricks, turning suddenly to spring. Not the tentative spring of early April, but a fine May day with balmy Caribbean breezes.

A battered VW beetle with Nebraska plates pulled up to the curb. The top was rolled back. In the midday sun, Heidi's pale hair was almost translucent.

Sarah noted her T-shirt and faded jeans. "I think I've overdressed."

"I've brought a change of clothes. Ken promised me a quick game of basketball."

"You?" Sarah glanced at the thin arms resting on the steering wheel. "I wouldn't have tapped you for a jock."

"Wrong again," said Heidi cheerfully, pulling into the traffic on Pennsylvania Avenue. "Star of my high school basketball team. And we made it to the state semifinals. I learned from my brother. Only I learned too well. Got so I could beat him one-on-one. Then he lost interest."

They drove down the ramp to Rock Creek Parkway, almost empty on the holiday. By the side of the road, the creek burbled cheerfully, sparkling in the sunlight.

"Why do you keep the Nebraska tags?" Sarah asked. "You haven't lived there for years."

"I'll be going back. And insurance is a lot cheaper in Nebraska than in D.C."

"You're going to live in Nebraska?" This was difficult to imagine. "Is there a family business? Or a boyfriend?" Sarah was intrigued. Heidi's private life was a mystery.

"Family business?" Heidi laughed. "My dad's a mailman. And there's no boyfriend." She pointed suddenly at a tree. "Look at that cardinal. This city has good birds, I'll say that for it."

Sarah was puzzled. "So what's the plan? Are you going to work for a firm in Omaha?"

"Do I look that dumb? I figure that I can save a hundred thousand dollars in three years here. Then I'm going back to Omaha and set up a little antiques business. People back home have things in their attics that they drool over in Washington. It shouldn't be hard to make ends meet."

"I don't understand," said Sarah. "Why go to law school at all in that case? It seems a hard way to get together a little capital."

"Yeah, well capital is a new item in my family." Heidi adjusted her oversized sunglasses. "It was a big deal when I went to the state university. I wasn't awfully serious when I applied to law school. But when I got into Yale, it seemed impossible to say no. Anyhow, it was kind of a hoot."

Sarah considered the thousands of aspiring lawyers who would sacrifice several limbs of their family tree to be accepted to Yale. Kind of a hoot!

"You have to understand," said Heidi, "that for me Yale was sort of an extended anthropological field trip. I had never been out of the midwest. And there I was in the Ivy League with people like you, who got taken to Broadway shows for their sixth birthday."

"Eighth birthday in my case. And it was off-Broadway."

"Even worse."

Bradley was shooting baskets in his driveway. He introduced them to his wife, Angelica, a statuesque beauty nearly as tall as himself. Angelica, Sarah knew, was a rising star at *Time*. Sarah could only imagine the level of determination required to achieve this kind of success in a white male hierarchy.

But if Angelica felt the strain, it was not apparent. While Bradley and Heidi bobbed and matched layups, Sarah followed Angelica into the kitchen. Angelica calmly slipped the salmon en croute into the oven and let Sarah help with the place settings. Angelica's concern seemed to be reserved for her husband.

"I will thank God when this partnership vote is over," she declared. "Personally, I think it would be a blessing if they ask Ken to leave. From what I can see, things at that firm never improve. Even the partners work like dogs. But either way, I'll be happy just to have the agony over with."

"Is he taking it that bad?" Sarah asked, setting down a wine glass.

"No, not there." Angelica smiled. "That's where the kids will sit. Strictly Flintstones stemware for them." She glanced at Sarah. "So what did all of you think of Felix Wolfson? His death is going to be listed in our Milestones column. Of course," she added, "it's a slow news week."

"What did we think?" Sarah wondered what Angelica had in mind. "He was very brilliant. Some people considered him the best litigator in town. And he was pretty intolerable. A lot of people could agree on that."

"That's interesting," said Angelica noncommittally. The five-year-old twins rushed through the door, clamoring about some point that Sarah couldn't quite make out.

"Absolutely not," said Angelica, and the two girls were instantly silent. "Now come and say hello."

"They're adorable," said Sarah sincerely when the twins had rushed up the stairs to retrieve another Christmas present.

"Thank you." Angelica laughed. "We try to keep from spoiling them. I'm not always sure we succeed."

Bradley and Heidi came in for a quick shower and Sarah found herself drawn into an inscrutable computer game with the twins. By the time they were seated at the table, Sarah was already exhausted. How did mothers cope? Angelica's gracious calm seemed even more impressive.

Dinner conversation focused for a time on the children's Christmas. Santa Claus was alleged to have made an early-morning appearance, and the descriptions of his bounty were enthusiastic. Only Bradley refused to join in the spirit of the day, fending off questions with curt monosyllables.

"Forgive my husband," said Angelica. "It's been so long since we've had people over for dinner that he's forgotten how to be a host."

"I think Ken's still recovering from our game," Heidi declared. "Just admit that the better woman won."

Bradley bestirred himself and flashed his broad smile. "I'll admit that much." He contemplated a forkful of salmon. "I'm sorry if I'm a little out of it. Work's got me down."

"So what else is new?" asked Sarah.

Bradley shook his head. "It's different this time. I keep thinking, how did I ever get myself into this mess?"

"What mess?" asked Sarah.

"The partnership vote," answered Heidi. "Strictly a no-win proposition."

"It would be for you," Sarah responded, "since you have no intention of staying at the firm. It's different for Ken."

"Is it?" said Bradley. He swiveled to face her, fork and knife clenched tightly in his powerful hands. "What makes you so sure? For eight years my sole professional goal has been my apotheosis to the letterhead of Arant and Devries. Now I feel as though I've been trapped in a long, complicated nightmare. And I don't know how to get out."

For a moment there was silence. Angelica excused the twins until dessert.

"If you want to leave, honey, there are plenty of other jobs." Angelica patted her husband on the arm. "You're not exactly unemployable."

"I don't need to be told that," said Bradley sharply. "But working at a place like Arant gets to you. Little by little you buy into their conception of the good life. And when it's time to leave, you discover you've become one of them."

"Come on," said Sarah, "this is all a little somber, isn't it? You don't have to decide your future right now. You've got to be a shoo-in for partnership."

Bradley shook his head. "You can never be certain. There are three other associates up for partnership. And the firm has never made more than two partners in a year."

"Ah," mused Heidi, "the four survivors of a class of twenty-five who struggle to the pot of gold at the finish line."

"But look at the cases you've worked on," Sarah urged. "You've been the workhorse of Forrest Labs. They couldn't go to trial without you. And what about the Deauville trial? The biggest coup of the year."

Angelica shook her head. "I've never been happy about the Deauville trial. Ken told me about that other woman—the one the prosecution tried to put on the stand. I've always wondered what the verdict would have been if she had testified."

This was a question Sarah had asked herself a hundred times in the last three months. "Maybe the result would have been different," she said. "But that's why we have rules of evidence in the first place—because it's easy to convict defendants on the basis of inference and innuendo. A prosecutor wouldn't need to prove any specific crime beyond a reasonable doubt. The jury would figure that the defendant must be guilty of *something*."

"Oh, I know that," Angelica replied. "I just couldn't believe that both women could be lying."

"All the more reason," said Heidi, "to congratulate Deauville's lawyers." She laughed. "Maybe a partnership at Arant and Devries is an appropriate reward for Ken after all."

"Thanks for the kind thought," said Bradley.

Angelica stood to clear the table, brushing away offers of help. "Get the firm gossip out of your system," she said. "When I come back we can have a civilized conversation."

"You know," said Heidi, pouring herself another glass of wine, "I was reading the transcript of the Deauville trial the other night."

"You were *what?*" said Sarah incredulously. "Is that your idea of fun?"

"Well, it was more fun than the interrogatories I was working on. It makes good reading. Remember the part when Fallon suddenly tells the judge that Irene Shaughnessy released herself from a sanatorium?"

"I'm not likely to forget it," said Sarah.

"Neither is the prosecutor," Heidi said. "That's what's so interesting when you see it in print: the prosecutor was totally blown away by the news." She took a swallow of wine. "It just doesn't make sense."

"What doesn't?" said Bradley. "That the prosecutor didn't know about the sanatorium? But why should she? Irene Shaughnessy didn't want people to know about her alcoholism. There was no reason for her to tell the U.S. Attorney about it."

"Could be," said Heidi, "but our investigator discovered the truth. Who was he? Superman? Why was the government in the dark? I mean, this wasn't some routine drug case. This was big time."

"They probably couldn't afford investigators," said Bradley. "Or not very good ones. Government litigation operates on a shoestring."

Angelica placed a strawberry shortcake on the table.

"That's homemade," said Heidi ecstatically. "I haven't seen anything look so good since I left Nebraska."

"Taste it first," said Angelica.

The twins surged back at the news of dessert. Bradley seemed to shake off his gloom and opened a bottle of champagne to accompany the cake. Outside, the sun was already beginning to set.

Bradley raised a glass: "As Tiny Tim would say, Merry Christmas and God bless us all, everyone."

Chapter 30

For at least a few minutes, Fallon felt as though it were a perfect Christmas. Streaming along on the motorcycle, with the wind in his face and his daughter's arms around his waist, he enjoyed a rare interlude of unreflective contentment.

After they crossed the Chain Bridge into Virginia, the suburbs gave way to country estates. This was horse country. High walls sheltered vast grounds and invisible mansions. At an unmarked gate flanked by two stone lions, Fallon turned up a curving drive beneath rows of ancient sycamores. After several twists, the trees gave way to carefully tended lawns and the mellow brick portico of Waverly Hill.

Fallon parked his bike beside a low-slung Jaguar and helped Molly out of her helmet.

"Is this a park?" she whispered. "I thought we were going to someone's house."

"I guess it's a park all right," said Fallon. "But it belongs to someone in my office. His family have owned it for generations."

"They must be awfully rich." Molly looked about with evident awe.

"They sure are," said Fallon. "But don't say anything about it when we're inside."

"Daddy!" Molly was exasperated. "How old do you think I am?"

She soon forgot her annoyance at the sight of the butler who opened the door. Overcome, Molly followed the butler into a vast, high-ceilinged room. Two dozen or so guests were scattered in small knots. Devries rolled over to greet them.

"Peter, I'm glad you could make it. This must be Molly. The last time I saw you, you had just learned how to talk."

"How do you do," said Molly politely.

Fallon grinned.

"We had a most remarkable gathering here last night," said Devries. "A party for all the children of the Roosevelt cabinet. One strange character stood in that corner all evening uttering barely a word. Couldn't figure out who he was. I wondered later if he might the illegitimate progeny of Frances Perkins."

"Enough of this." Charlotte Devries placed a hand on Molly's shoulder. "Molly will be bored stiff if she stays in this room one more minute." Charlotte wore a flowing dress of gray silk and a necklace of large, luminescent pearls. Fallon had not seen her since his discovery of the photograph. He looked quickly away.

"I'm going to take Molly out to the stables and fix her up with a pony," Charlotte announced.

"The stables?" Molly was wide-eyed. "You have horses right here?"

Charlotte laughed. "Pretty close." She turned to Fallon. "Don't worry, Peter. A fine young man who works in the stables will be keeping an eye on Molly."

"Make life easy for him," said Fallon. "Do what he tells you."

Molly gave him a conspiratorial wink and followed Charlotte out of the room.

Devries led Fallon to French doors opening out onto a broad terrace. The bar had been set up outdoors. Fallon asked for Dr Pepper, settled for a 7-up.

Devries caught his arm in his pincer grip. "Peter, I don't think you've met Jeff Unruh?" A short, balding man who might have been a body double for Felix Wolfson stuck out a plump hand. Fallon looked curiously into the eyes of the CEO of Forrest Labs. The resemblance to Wolfson ended right there. The contrast between the dull gaze and Wolfson's gleaming intelligence was startling.

"I've been looking forward to meeting you," said Unruh. "Tragedy about Wolfson."

Fallon nodded.

"From what I hear, you're the man of the hour. How do you see our trial shaping up?

Fallon had absolutely no idea. He knew next to nothing about the case he was taking over. This would hardly be reassuring to a CEO looking at a potential billion-dollar liability. Fallon launched into a confident exposition on techniques for handling expert witnesses, studded with references to half a dozen of his major victories. Unruh was visibly impressed. Fallon was glad Molly wasn't around.

"You know," said Unruh, "I've been wanting to meet you ever since the Deauville trial. That was quite a triumph." He reached over to the bar and ordered another gin and tonic. "What about you," he said, pointing at Fallon's 7-up. "The same?"

"No thanks."

"When I read about your performance, I thought: that's the man I want for my lawyer. If he can get Cicero Deauville off the hook, taking care of Forrest Labs will be child's play." Unruh leaned forward confidentially. "Tell me the truth, was he guilty?"

It occurred to Fallon that Unruh had been drinking most of the afternoon. He looked more closely at the CEO's eyes. Yes, that was it. Unruh would imbibe steadily till he hit the sack. His speech would remain fluent and unslurred. But the eyes would grow ever more remote. Fallon knew all about this sort of thing.

"We need to set up a meeting early in the New Year," said Fallon. "There's a lot to talk about."

Unruh chuckled. "Don't blame you for not answering my question. Lawyers are paid to be discreet. It's good to know I can trust you."

Fallon spotted Charlotte Devries across the terrace. He excused himself.

"Can we go somewhere to talk?"

Charlotte showed no surprise. Without a word, she led him

indoors and into a book-lined study. Despite the unseasonable weather, a fire crackled in the hearth.

"I have to talk to you about Wolfson," said Fallon.

"For heaven's sake, Peter, if you must look so serious, please take a seat. Voltaire once said that you can turn any tragedy into a comedy just by sitting down."

"I'll sit down then," said Fallon. "But I don't think you'll find what I have to say amusing. I've found the photograph."

Charlotte nodded calmly. The announcement appeared to be a matter of utter indifference. But a deep blush slowly spread up from her neck. She looked more beautiful than ever.

"Were you looking for the photograph that night in Wolfson's office?" Fallon asked.

Charlotte sighed. "It was just a desperate hope. I was sure he'd have it under lock and key."

"Was he blackmailing you?"

"Of course not." The matter-of-fact tone was convincing. Was it too well rehearsed? Fallon was unsure.

"Had you asked Wolfson to return the photo?"

"The subject never came up. But I thought of it immediately when I learned he was dead. I was afraid it might fall into the wrong hands."

"So only you and Wolfson knew the photo existed?"

"Haven't I made that clear? I don't see what you're driving at." Charlotte looked at Fallon defiantly. "Have you come to pass judgment on a shameless whore?"

Fallon shrugged. This, too, had the sound of a scripted line. "Your life is none of my business. But I'm the executor of Wolfson's estate and someone has broken into his office. I thought it might have been you looking for the picture."

"A theft? What did they take?"

"I don't know. I was hoping you could tell me."

"Well, I can't."

There was silence in the room. A log shifted in the fireplace.

"Are you going to give me the photograph?" asked Charlotte finally.

"Eventually."

"Should I ask why you're holding on to it? Or am I better off not imagining."

"No one will see it," said Fallon. "That includes me."

He began to stand up.

"Wait a moment," said Charlotte. She adopted a pleading tone. "I want you to understand something, Peter. I may not be an ideal wife, but I was always a faithful one. Until last year."

"You don't have to explain any of this to me," said Fallon.

"But I want to. You must understand how terribly St. John's accident affected our lives. He had always lived for the outdoors. Suddenly, he was confined to a wheelchair."

Charlotte looked down at her carefully manicured hands. "St. John grew very dependent on me. And he resented me for it. You can imagine how it was. So I was vulnerable when Felix made his move. He was so certain, so strong. It was like receiving an infusion of life."

"And St. John never suspected?"

"I'm sure he didn't. He would never have kept silent about his suspicions." Charlotte paused. "I know this is only a rationalization, but I think my relationship with Felix helped to protect St. John. It was clear to me that St. John had lost control of the firm. Wolfson might easily have decided to push him aside entirely. I think I helped to keep the peace between them."

What a schemer this woman was. Fallon recalled the long period of amicable relations between Wolfson and Devries. So Charlotte had been holding the firm together by sleeping with Wolfson.

Charlotte stood up. "As I say, I don't excuse myself. But I wanted you to know how things were."

Together they walked down to the stables. Fallon mulled over Charlotte's account of herself as a middle-aged Lady Chatterley with Wolfson as her gamekeeper. How much of it was true? Charlotte had delivered this speech for a reason. Who was she protecting?

Molly ran up as she saw him. Her face was radiant.

"Daddy. It was great! I want to have riding lessons. And Larry says I can come back and ride here any time."

A trim young man leading a pony into its stall grinned at Fallon.

"We'll talk to your mother," said Fallon. "She makes all the decisions."

"I see the afternoon has been a success after all." Charlotte smiled at father and daughter. She was, thought Fallon, a formidable woman.

Chapter 31

Christmas week, Sarah discovered, was something of a holiday even for those few who showed up for work. Attorneys roamed the halls in jeans, left early for long lunches, and hurried home at the start of the rush hour. The pace seemed comfortingly familiar and Sarah recalled with a smile that it was, after all, the typical routine of academia.

She was gazing idly at a time sheet on her desk, wondering how she would concoct some billable hours, when the phone rang. It was Sterling Gray.

"Jason came in with me this morning. Why not join us for lunch?" Sarah hadn't seen Sterling since the holiday. With some trepidation, she agreed. Gray brought his son down to the fifth floor. Sarah examined the face of the six-year-old for some trace of his father. None was apparent except (dammit) for the weak chin.

As they walked to the elevator, Heidi Hollings came around the corner.

"Where are you eating?" she demanded.

"I thought we'd go to Red Sage as a Christmas treat," Gray replied.

"Great," she said. "I've been wanting to try it."

"I'm afraid our reservation is only for three."

Heidi laughed. "Any table for three can hold four. Trust me, I waitressed in the best steak house in Omaha."

They were seated in the largest of the downstairs dining rooms, overlooking the open kitchen. Gray ordered a round of tart margaritas, the best Sarah could remember. Jason, against his father's advice, ordered a margarita without alcohol which he promptly rejected on receipt. Ignoring his complaints, Sarah surveyed the elaborate decor.

"Over in the chili bar," Gray informed Jason, "they have clouds that flash blue lightning."

"I was admiring the metal lizards on the door handles," said Heidi.

Gray set down his drink with an air of satisfaction. "Some people make fun of Red Sage for being so trendy. But I think it's great. I come whenever I can."

"Have you tried—" Sarah began.

"Daddy, what's butternut painted soup?"

Gray nodded approvingly at Jason. "That's a good question. Let's ask the waiter."

When the waiter arrived, Gray pointed at his son. "This young man has some questions about the menu."

The waiter smiled. "The butternut soup is exquisite—one side is golden squash, the other is inky black bean."

"Ugh." Jason closed his eyes in horror.

"You might prefer the oyster corn soup."

"There's nothing here I like."

The waiter laughed. "We have a very large menu. And if you don't see what you want, we can make it up for you specially."

"I want a hamburger."

"You can have a hamburger anywhere," Sterling put in. "Why not try something different? How about some chili? I know you like chili."

Jason shook his head and swiveled on his chair, turning his back on his father.

Sarah skipped the appetizer and watched while Heidi tackled the sage-flavored buffalo sausage with sweet pepper relish. Sterling went for the organic greens dressed with jalapeño buttermilk vinaigrette.

Jason launched into rambling story. Eventually Sarah realized that the child was recounting an evening with his mother in a

Paris nightclub. Sarah tried, without success, to imagine her own mother hauling her young children off to sample nightlife in the Montmartre.

"Did you read that there's going to be a Cabinet shakeup?" Heidi asked.

"Daddy!" Jason interrupted. "Mommy says the skis you gave me aren't the right kind."

"What does she mean, not the right kind?"

"That's what she said. She said they're the wrong make and we should take them back."

"You tell your mommy she doesn't know what she's talking about." Gray's face had grown red. "She's never been on skis in her life," he said to Sarah.

The waiter arrived with their main courses.

"What's that?" asked Jason, pointing at Sarah's plate.

"It's trout. See, Heidi has that, too."

"I want some."

"Sure," said Gray. He leaned over and scooped a bite of the cornmeal-crusted trout from Sarah's dish. "Try that."

"I want that," said Jason.

"Honey, you've ordered your hamburger." Gray pointed at Jason's plate encouragingly. "It looks delicious. Have a bite."

"I want hers!"

"You can have hers some other time."

"Now!"

Heidi slid her plate across the table. "Take mine. I lost my appetite." She beckoned to the waiter. "How about another margarita?"

"So what did you think of the little brat?" Heidi asked when they were back at the firm.

"He wasn't so bad," said Sarah defensively. "He probably just has problems with strangers."

Heidi laughed. "Is this a psychologist speaking? That child revels in power. They should put *him* in the Cabinet."

"It's not easy when your parents are divorced. Any kid could get screwed up."

"Oh, I'm sure he comes by it honestly." Heidi stood and stretched. "Now I'll be hungry the rest of the day."

"I'll run out to get a sandwich with you," Sarah offered.

Heidi giggled. "I hope the mustard greens and green chiles keep the brat awake all night."

"I don't think he actually ate enough to make a difference."

"I suppose not." Heidi shook her head, sending her delicate hair flying. "Honestly, is that kid really worth bankrupting yourself for?"

"What do you mean?

Heidi's pale eyebrows raised. "Didn't you know? It was a very nasty custody battle. Sterling flipped when his wife ran off with Dick Llewellyn, the former Secretary of State. He must have thought she was trading up in the marriage department. Sterling hired a lot of high-priced talent to keep Jason. It didn't work, and Sterling still owes lawyers' fees. Quelle irony."

"The poor guy," said Sarah. "I had no idea."

"I think I'll get in a couple of billable hours," said Heidi. "Are you going to go out running later?"

"If it's not too cold."

"I'll stop by your office. We can bill our run to Forrest Labs."

Chapter 32

The next morning Sarah was wandering idly through the library stacks when her name was paged.

When she arrived in Fallon's office, she found a scene that trivialized his customary untidiness. Heaps of files had been stacked on every available desk and tabletop. Fallon, dressed in jeans and a flannel shirt, squatted on the floor, surrounded by a semicircle of paper.

Sarah sat down on the floor beside him. "How was your Christmas?"

"Molly had fun, which was good enough for me. Christmas, as they say, is for children. The rest of us just seek to endure. How about you?"

"Heidi and I had dinner at Ken's. His kids are great."

"How is Ken doing?" Fallon asked. "He's seemed a little jumpy lately."

"His wife thinks he's a nervous wreck about the partnership decision. I told her not to worry. I was sure you guys would do the right thing."

"Did Ken say anything about the vote?"

"No. Just exhibited a little weltschmerz."

Fallon sighed. "Speaking of weltschmerz, or schmerz generally, we received a new discovery request from the government in the West Bank case."

Sarah could feel the holiday spirit draining away. "So the moving finger of fate has pointed to me?"

"In the great lottery of life, you have turned up a losing ticket." Fallon gestured at the avalanche of paper all around him. "I'm trying to read my way into Forrest Labs. So you're going to have to take the first cut at a response in West Bank. The government is on a fishing expedition. They want a ton of documents. We'll negotiate to see if we can cut the request down to reasonable proportions. But first we have to get our arguments on each request nailed down."

"Big job," said Sarah resignedly.

"And almost everyone's away. But I've spoken to Heidi and she can give you a hand. At least you'll be working with a friend."

Sarah recalled the evening that Heidi first stepped into her office in the middle of the Deauville trial. The chances then that she would come to think of the impertinent stranger as a friend would have seemed bleak.

"Heidi was holding forth on the Deauville trial at Christmas dinner," Sarah said. "She couldn't understand why you had all the inside dope on Irene Shaughnessy while the government was caught flat-footed."

"Did you enlighten her?"

"How? I was as shocked as everyone else in the courtroom. I was out of the loop. Who was the miracle private investigator anyway?"

Fallon scratched his head. "To tell the truth, I don't remember. I'm not sure I ever knew. Wolfson was handling that." He stood up. "But it's easy enough to find out."

They walked down the hall to Wolfson's door. Fallon produced two keys for the double set of locks installed after the break-in. Reaching into the walnut cabinet, he pulled out a stack of folders.

"Wolfson's personal files on the Deauville case," Fallon explained. He seated himself at the desk and spread out the papers. "The investigator's reports are sure to be here."

But Fallon was wrong. "I don't get it," he muttered. "Here are Wolfson's notes for the Andrea Callas cross. Here's your

privilege memo. Ken's memo on use of force. But nothing from
the investigator."

"He might have kept the investigator's reports separately,"
Sarah suggested.

"Well here's his name anyway," said Fallon, "writ large on his
bill. Maurice Politz, Poydras Street in New Orleans. I wonder
how Wolfson found him."

"What are all those question marks?"

"Wolfson seems to be questioning the items on his bill. But I
can't see why. It looks to me like Maurice was a bargain. Especially judging by results."

Sarah stifled a yawn thinking of the afternoon ahead. She had
no enthusiasm for another round in West Bank. It was just like
the government to stir up trouble during the holidays.

"I'll call the file room to see if Wolfson sent any Deauville
materials to storage." Fallon lifted the receiver, then studied the
phone. "I think Wolfson had some gadget installed to record
his calls."

Sarah peered over his shoulder. "I thought that was illegal."

Fallon turned the phone upside down. "I'm not sure how this
damn thing works. Hold on a moment." He called in Fran Rendelman, still in black. Sarah wondered how long the secretary's
mourning would continue. "Oh, no," she said when Fallon had
explained the problem. "Mr. Wolfson didn't tape phone calls."

"That's a relief," said Fallon.

"Mr. Wolfson taped conversations that took place here in
the office."

"Are you kidding?" Sarah exclaimed. "Like the Nixon tapes?"

"Not at all." Rendelman glared at her disapprovingly. "The
President's tapes were voice-activated. Mr. Wolfson taped only
select conversations."

Sarah glanced at Fallon who seemed to have difficulty digesting this new information.

"So Wolfson didn't tape conversations routinely," he said.

"I wouldn't think so," said Rendelman. "Every few weeks he'd
have me take out one tape and put a new tape in. But I couldn't
say how many conversations he actually stored on each tape."

"What did you do with the tapes you removed?"

"The really old ones we threw out or sent to storage. The rest were kept right here in the office." Rendelman walked over to the walnut cabinet and crouched down to reach the bottom shelf.

After a methodical search, she looked back over her shoulder. "I'm sure I don't understand," she said. "The tapes were always kept right here."

Fallon sank back in Wolfson's chair and gazed vacantly at the ceiling. Sarah wondered how many of her own conversations had been stored away on the tape? Who would have thought that Wolfson was even more reprehensible than he seemed?

After a minute or two Fallon sat upright and focused on Rendelman. "Is there still a tape in the machine?"

"If you'll wait," she said primly, "I'll check."

She went outside to her desk and returned with a small key. "The actual recording mechanism is in this antique music box," she said proudly, as if she had installed the device. Inserting the key into the delicately carved box, she pulled open the lid and withdrew a tape cassette. "Here you are."

"Thanks," said Fallon, pocketing the tape. "It seems as though Felix Wolfson had quite a bundle of tricks up his sleeve."

"Oh yes indeed," said Rendelman with a catch in her voice. "There was no one like him."

Chapter 33

When Sarah broke the news over lunch at the Childe Harolde, the reactions could hardly have been more different. Heidi burst out laughing.

"You're right," she said. "It was just like Nixon."

"My father always said that Nixon was the devil put on earth to test the American people," said Sarah.

"Maybe Wolfson was the devil," Heidi agreed. "He was certainly clever enough."

"He was a bastard," said Ken Bradley. The suppressed fury in his voice made Sarah shrink back in her seat. "Sleazy and unethical."

"But not illegal," said Heidi.

"Oh, no," said Bradley. "Felix Wolfson could commit his crimes without breaking the law."

Heidi patted his hand. "Don't take it personally."

"I wonder what kinds of things he recorded," Sarah mused. "Negotiations? Confidential client meetings?"

"Why don't you ask Fallon?" said Bradley bitterly. "It sounds as though he's got the evidence."

"For all we know, there's nothing on the tape," Sarah reminded him.

"I'm sure we'll find out," said Bradley.

They lapsed into silence. Eventually, Heidi picked up as if

nothing had been said. "Did you know that the Childe Harolde used to be a club? Bruce Springsteen played here in the seventies before Dupont Circle went upscale."

Sarah looked around. It was hard to imagine the Boss in the Childe Harold. "Who provided this bit of musical trivia?"

"Peter Fallon. He and his wife lived in a group house at 19th and R when they first came to Washington. Can you imagine a group house in this area? Gone with the condos."

Sarah felt unreasonably slighted that Fallon should be imparting his personal history to Heidi Hollings. It was odd to think of Fallon as married. And in a group house!

For the first time during Christmas week, they cut lunch short to get back to work. Together, Sarah and Heidi teased out the convoluted sentences of the government's document request.

"Look at this one," said Heidi. "Number 108. 'Each and every document, tape or electronic transcription pertaining to or generated by the acquisition of West Bank stock by Donald Anderson, including but not limited to all correspondence, memoranda, certificates, and receipts issued by or to any person.' Jesus Christ."

"Let's split the requests down the middle," said Sarah. "I'll take 1 through 60. You take 61 through 120."

"Fair enough." Heidi headed for the door. "Last one finished buys the drinks."

Sarah gazed out the window at the fading light. The gray sky matched her mood. What was she doing here, she wondered? It was all right for Heidi. She was only twenty-three. In three years she'd be back in Nebraska running a prosperous antiques business. Probably be happily married to a handsome young man of good midwestern stock. And herself? She'd be thirty-three. Three years closer to partnership, knee-deep in memoranda, thrilled by the chance to take the occasional insignificant deposition.

Sarah threw her pencil across the room.

For the first time since the memorial service, Sarah remembered Fallon's theory about Wolfson's coffee. She recalled Fallon's questions that morning about Ken Bradley. Was it possible that Fallon suspected Ken? She thought uneasily of Bradley's disconcerting response to the news of Wolfson's tapes.

She got up to retrieve the pencil from the floor. This was absurd. Wolfson hadn't been murdered. And he certainly hadn't been murdered by Ken Bradley.

The phone rang.

"I told you it would be hard to get rid of me."

It was Cicero Deauville. Sarah sat down and took a deep breath.

"You there?" he asked.

"I was waiting for you to say something that deserved a response."

He laughed softly. "All right then. I'll give you something you can say yes to. How would you like to go out on New Year's Eve?"

Sarah was flattered. It was probably old-fashioned, but New Year's Eve still seemed like a special date.

"I'm busy."

"Don't play hard to get," said Deauville. "I have tickets for the Kennedy Center. Then a champagne buffet at Margot Kellerman's.

"I'm sorry, I already have a date." The regret was at least partly sincere. Margot Kellerman!

"Ah, well, I guess it's my fault," said Deauville. "You can't call a beautiful woman a day ahead of time and expect her to be free."

"I expect most women break their dates for you."

"They don't. And I wouldn't let them. We southerners have our faults, but we do have manners."

"I'm glad to hear it."

Deauville laughed again. "You're thawing. I can tell. Next time you'll melt."

There was a soft click. Sarah sat still for several seconds before slowly setting down the phone.

Chapter 34

"When did it begin?"

"Ask your wife."

"I have. She told me to ask you."

"Isn't that just like a woman." Wolfson laughed unpleasantly. "If it will satisfy your unhealthy curiosity, it began while you were still in the hospital."

The tape rolled silently for several seconds.

"That photograph is sickening."

"Shameless, isn't it?" Wolfson agreed. "Charlotte is quite the exhibitionist. I don't think I've ever met anyone so free of inhibitions. There's nothing she won't try. But I'm sure you remember."

"Why did you send it to me?"

"I took pity on you. St. John is living in a fool's paradise, I said to myself. I can open his eyes."

"You are a foul snake."

Wolfson chuckled. "Snakes are so underrated."

Silence again. Fallon took a sip of Dr Pepper and eyed the tape deck warily as if Wolfson were secreted within.

"What do you want?"

"Want?" protested Wolfson. "Why should I want anything? It seems I have everything already."

"Don't drag this out. I'm sure you relish the pain you're inflicting. That might be motivation enough. But I've known

123

you too long. Just come out with it so we can end this bloody farce."

"I've pointed out the problem to you before, St. John. Negotiations require patience. This sort of straight talk is for amateurs."

"Humor me," said Devries acidly.

"If you insist. I'll try and match your straight shooting. Resign."

"What?" It came out as a snarl.

"Was I too straight? How about 'take leave,' 'become of-counsel,' 'assume senior status.' Is that better?"

"This is my firm, Wolfson. And my father's, and my grandfather's."

"Yes, and Charlotte was your wife, too. Though I assume you didn't share her with your revered ancestors."

As Devries' voice rose to a scream, Fallon turned down the volume. He didn't want the neighbors calling the police.

Fallon recalled the morning of the murder. He and Bradley had stood in the door of the kitchenette. This would be the point at which the rising voices in Wolfson's office had caught their attention.

Sure enough, the confrontation was drawing to a close.

"Really, St. John, when will you learn that howls of rage don't carry the day? Be realistic. I have all the cards—your clients, your wife, her most appealing photograph. The script demands a graceful exit."

"I'll see you rot in hell."

"Don't be old-fashioned. Just think of this as a hostile takeover."

Back in third grade at St. Benedict's, Fallon had learned that eavesdropping was not just wrong. It was also a bad idea. "You can discover things you wish you'd never learned," Sister Claire explained.

Crossing Sister Claire had always been a mistake. Today was no exception. For a moment Fallon considered switching off the tape. He had heard quite enough. Instead, he allowed the second act of Wolfson's last drama to unfold.

Fallon heard the door open. A minute later he heard Wolfson

call to Bradley: "What the hell are you waiting for? I don't have all day."

"I brought the deposition outlines," said Bradley.

Wolfson was uninterested. "They can wait."

"I was up all night getting them ready for you."

"Really? Well, I do apologize. Perhaps we can find a way of cutting your work load."

"Impossible," said Bradley. "You know what the next few months will be like."

"Oh, I agree. This trial will be all-consuming. It would leave you no time at all for sending out résumés."

Fallon could actually hear the intake of breath.

"What are you getting at?"

"I think you know."

"Just say it."

Wolfson was amused. "Come right out with it, eh? That seems to be the theme of the day. Everyone wants it straight. No sugar-coating. Well, I always try to oblige. What I'm trying to tell you, Ken, is that your future lies elsewhere. A partnership at Arant and Devries is not in the cards."

"Why the hell not?" The effort at self-restraint was almost palpable.

"Why not? Because you just don't cut it. You're reasonably bright, you work hard, but there's no spark, no originality. And after eight years, Ken, there's not the hint of a client."

"That's ridiculous," said Bradley. He was deliberately speaking slowly, measuring out each word. "No associate has brought in any clients to speak of. What's going on? I want specifics."

"And you shall have them." Fallon heard the crackle of paper. "This is my report. It details my views. You'll receive a copy when it goes to the partnership. And, of course, you'll have an opportunity to respond. Due process and all that."

"Where's this coming from?" said Bradley. "My evaluations have never mentioned a lack of 'originality.' "

"Great expectations? I don't doubt you've nourished them. And, perhaps, you may have thought that affirmative action con-siderations might have helped your cause. But you're wrong. This is strictly a meritocracy."

"Meritocracy?" For the first time, Bradley's voice rose to a shout. "How can you sit there and feed me that bullshit? This is an ass-licking, back-stabbing pool of sharks."

"You're mixing your metaphors. That always makes a bad impression."

The door opened and slammed shut. For another minute the tape whirred on silently. Then it clicked off.

Fallon took his glass of Dr Pepper to the window. He gazed unseeing at the lights of the Kennedy Center. Bradley, or Devries, or Charlotte must have known of Wolfson's tapes, broken in to retrieve them. But they had missed the last cassette, the joker in the pack.

The telephone rang. It was his old friend Kara Melnik. Fallon had judged her the best forensic pathologist around, back when he was prosecuting the Tozzi murders.

"Did you get my report?" Kara asked.

"Almost a week ago."

"I sent it over right before I left. Handed it to the messenger and hopped a cab to the airport. Miami at Christmas is awful."

"Never been there," said Fallon. "Never been in Florida for that matter."

"You live a charmed life. So did you follow up? Any reason I should have found that digitoxin in Wolfson's tissue?"

"I called Wolfson's doctor," said Fallon. "Wolfson was taking digitoxin for a heart condition."

"Oh." Kara sounded disappointed. "So we have a legitimate cause of death. When I found the digitoxin I had my hopes up. We don't get that many poison cases anymore." She sighed.

"Tricky thing, though, digitoxin," Kara continued. "I mean, take it in the right dosage and you control heart irregularities. But take a bit extra and you get cardiac arrest." Kara grew more cheerful contemplating the renewed possibility of foul play.

"So which was it?" Fallon asked. "Was it just a prescribed dosage? Or is there that fatal bit extra?"

"I'll have to double-check my notes." Kara pondered the problem. "But I don't think I'll be able to say for sure. A fatal dose would be maybe four times the amount of the prescribed amount. But once it spreads through the bloodstream and has time to be absorbed, it's difficult to diagnose with certainty. I'd just be guessing."

"I guess that nails it down."

Kara laughed. "Come on, Fallon. You know how these things work. This isn't TV. You want certainties, call Quincy."

"I'll tell you what. I'll throw you a softball to make you feel better. Let's assume death was the result of an overdose of digitoxin. And let's assume that the killer slipped it to Wolfson in powder form. How long would it be from ingestion till death?"

"Yeah, that's easier. Of course, you can't be certain, but I'd say at least an hour."

"See, I knew you could do it."

Kara giggled. "Come back to the government, Fallon. I can't keep doing your work at taxpayer expense."

"I may do that."

"And give up that dough? I'll believe it when I see it. What are you doing for New Year's?"

"New Year's Day? I'm taking my kid to the zoo."

"No, idiot. New Year's Eve."

"Nothing. I hate New Year's Eve. I get into bed with a book at nine and make sure I'm asleep by eleven."

"Very sociable. Why don't you come to my place? Some of the guys are coming over."

"The cadaver crew from the lab? No thanks. I'll stick to my book."

"There'll be some single women. If I can't catch you myself, I can at least fix you up."

Fallon laughed. "Have a happy New Year, Dr. Melnik. And thanks."

Fallon picked up his Dr Pepper. The morning of Wolfson's death was vivid in his mind. The lawyers moved in and out of Wolfson's office like characters in a play. Enter Devries. Exit Devries. Enter Bradley. Exit Bradley. Enter Strasser. Scream.

But if Wolfson had consumed the poison at least an hour before his death, this script was irrelevant. The powdered digitoxin, mixed into the Barrister Blend, was ready to do its work whenever Wolfson brewed his last cup of coffee.

In his mind's eye, Fallon saw St. John Devries, red with fury.

Ken Bradley gripping the arms of his chair to keep his temper in check. Charlotte Devries, smiling as she lay splayed out on Wolfson's bed.

Fallon switched off the track lighting. He had come to a decision. He would let Wolfson's murder lie. He would not destroy another life to avenge Wolfson's death. The Wolfson file was closed.

Chapter 35

Sterling had elected to ring in the New Year at the Auberge Chez François. Several miles out of the town, it was the sort of place where anxious young men proposed matrimony and mature couples celebrated anniversaries. Sarah, a New Yorker at heart, preferred noisy little restaurants where spectacular food was accepted as matter of course. But, as she admitted, Washington was not long on brilliant bistros.

As the evening edged toward midnight, it became obvious that something was wrong. It was not the food. The Alsace duck was moist and savory, the Riesling full and fruity. Sterling insisted on ordering a second bottle. It was not even their fellow diners—the usual well-heeled crew of lawyers and consultants.

So what was wrong? Sarah found her thoughts wandering to Cicero Deauville at the Kennedy Center. And even to Peter Fallon doing God knows what for his New Year's Eve. Sterling Gray, sitting across the table, seemed a virtual stranger.

Which was all the more terrible because Sterling had decided to unburden his heart. Despite Sarah's efforts at diversion, Sterling insisted on dissecting the horrors of his marriage and divorce. With perverse attention to detail, he recalled the evening he had arrived home to find his wife and her lover, surrounded by packed suitcases. Sterling had gone berserk. While he traded

ineffectual punches with the former Secretary of State, his wife
departed with their son.

"I don't mind telling you," Sterling said, taking a sip of dessert
wine, "that I was nearly at the end of my rope. For years I had
done all the right things, made all the right moves. Then my
perfect marriage became a perfect hell. And the job . . ." He let
the thought go unfinished and emptied his glass. Sarah realized
that he had consumed close to two bottles.

"But you turned it around," said Sarah with brittle cheer-
fulness. "And a great year lies ahead."

Sterling's hand closed around hers. "I think you're right."

The lights went off. For a moment they remained in darkness.
Then waiters, waving glittering sparklers, spread through the
room. Corks popped. The New Year had arrived.

Sterling moved around the table to kiss her. Sarah felt empty.
What was wrong with her? she wondered. This poor man obviously loved her. Was it too much for her to accept?

They drank champagne and sipped Courvoisier, and by the
time they reached the car, Sterling was weaving perceptibly.

"Do you really think you ought to be driving?" Sarah asked
as he slid behind the wheel.

"Did you ever read *Babbitt*? Great book. Babbitt says that the
last thing to go when a man gets drunk is his ability to drive a
car. It's an ingrained pattern of behavior."

Apparently Babbitt was right. Gray negotiated the winding
roads without difficulty and parked a few steps from the entrance
to Sarah's building. The doorman, who looked as though he had
been toasting the New Year himself, showed them to the elevator
with a flourish.

In the apartment, Sterling dropped his coat on the floor and
took her in his arms.

"I have a question to ask you."

A warning sounded in Sarah's head.

"No questions tonight, Sterling. Let's get into bed."

"One question first. I insist."

Sarah forced a smile. "All right, but make it quick."

Sterling took a step back and held her hands in his.

"Will you marry me?"

She had sensed it was coming. But it was worse than she had imagined.

"Now I know you're drunk," she said. "Let's get you to bed before you say things you'll regret."

Sterling stood still. "I'm serious."

Sarah kissed him gently. "Not now. Let's not be serious now."

"Are you saying no?"

"I'm saying we shouldn't talk about it now."

Sterling turned on his heel and sat heavily on the couch. "I don't think I can stand it," he said. "I've counted on you."

Oh, my God, thought Sarah. *A vin triste.*

"Don't be maudlin," she said sharply. "You're tired and you've had too much to drink."

Sterling rested his face in his hands. "I knew I shouldn't have asked you tonight. I knew I was rushing things." He looked up. "But neither of us is a teenager. At our age you can tell if it's going to work. So why wait?"

Sarah sat down on the couch and put an arm around him. "Come to bed, Sterling. I mean it. When you get to our age you also know that sometimes it's better to just shut up."

Sterling smiled bitterly. "You're good at this, aren't you? The benevolent Doctor Strasser. I see I'm guilty of a serious misconception. I'm sorry to have presumed on your affections."

Sarah stood up. "Don't be ridiculous. I'm just not ready to talk about marriage."

He looked up at her. "Tell me there's a chance you'll say yes."

"I can't do that. We'll just have to see how things work out."

"For Chrissakes." Sterling struggled to his feet. "Give me some hope."

Sarah took a step back. "We always have a good time together," she said lamely.

Sterling hung his head. For a moment Sarah thought he would pass out. Then she realized he was looking for his coat. When he found it, he headed for the door.

She ran after him. "You can't leave like this, Sterling. For God's sake, just come to bed. In the morning I'll make you pancakes."

"I think I'll leave while I still have my dignity."

He opened the door and walked down the hall. For a moment, Sarah thought she might follow. Then she heard the sound of the elevator closing.

Outside on the balcony, a sharp wind made her teeth chatter. In the distance she could hear the noise of raucous party goers on M Street. Another year was beginning. Her fourth decade stretched out before her.

She stepped back inside and looked around at the empty apartment. She heard a choking noise and realized, impersonally, that she had sobbed. A shudder wracked her body. She calmly sat on the couch and let the tears come.

Part 3

Chapter 36

Sarah returned to work invigorated by a passel of resolutions. It was time to make a new beginning. Felix Wolfson, the omnipresent ogre, was gone. The misguided romance with Sterling Gray was over. She was young, intelligent, attractive, and hauling in the bucks. In time, all prayers would be answered.

Buoyed by her own pep talk, Sarah threw herself into the thankless task of responding to the government's discovery request in the West Bank case. Working fourteen-hour days, she waded through documents, compiled objections, and drafted memos. In only five days she marched into Heidi's office, tired but triumphant.

"I think we made a little bet," she said. "Last one to finish buys the drinks. Where are you taking me?"

Heidi smiled. "Why don't we call it a draw? I finished yesterday."

Sarah flung herself into a chair, exasperated. "How did you do it? Pulling all-nighters?"

Heidi shrugged her thin shoulders. Her cornflower-blue eyes twinkled. "You've met your match, Strasser." She came around from behind her desk to sit next to her. "So how are you feeling?"

Sarah looked at her sharply. "What do you mean?"

"Lovers parting, that sort of thing."

Sarah sat up angrily. "Did he talk to you?"

"Calm down," said Heidi. "Nobody talked to me. But I see you. I see him. I make inferences. Haven't you ever heard of deduction?"

Sarah stared at her incredulously. "Are you some kind of witch?"

"Open eyes. Brain in order. No witchcraft there." Heidi stood up. "Let's find Fallon." As Sarah followed her down the hall she remembered Sterling saying that Heidi might be the most brilliant new associate in years. At the time Sarah had thought he was trying to tweak her. Now she reassessed the conversation.

It was already eight, but Fallon was still buried in Forrest Labs. On the floor of his office, the individual stacks of folders had disappeared, lost in an undifferentiated sea of paper. Sarah had barely seen Fallon since the New Year. She longed to tell him of her breakup with Sterling Gray. But, of course, this was impossible. Anyway, Fallon himself seemed unaccustomedly remote and preoccupied.

They picked a trail through the papers before discovering that there was no place to sit. All the chairs and the sturdy chesterfield were covered with files. Fallon looked up from the floor.

"West Bank?"

"Done," said Sarah. She held out their memos.

Fallon stretched out a hand, then stood up. "Better not leave anything in this office. It will never resurface again. Let's get out of this mess."

Out in the hall, Fallon scanned the memos. For ten minutes he read with total absorption, saying nothing. When he finished, he enveloped them both with his toothy grin. "Great work. I can't believe you turned this around so quickly."

"A little friendly competition," said Sarah.

"Well, I won't ask who won. I'll set up a meeting with Nat Zeldin tomorrow. We'll go down to the U.S. Attorney's office. Zeldin would never admit it, but that will win us some brownie points."

Heidi accompanied Sarah back to the fifth floor. Both of them avoided glancing at Felix Wolfson's office, still locked shut. Sarah wondered if she could safely mention Fallon's idea about Wolfson's coffee. Would he still want her to keep mum?

She had just decided that a promise was a promise, when Heidi broke in on her thoughts. "I get the creeps every time I go by Wolfson's office. I suppose it's even worse for you."

"I try not to think about it."

"You think they'll ever catch him?"

Sarah wasn't sure she had heard right. "Who?"

"Whoever killed him."

"Oh, no," she groaned. "Not you, too."

"Me too, what?"

"You, too, are a lunatic. You and Peter Fallon. He also had an idea about foul play, but he's dropped it. Thought someone had slipped poison into Wolfson's coffee."

Heidi clapped her hands together excitedly. "That's it. That must be how it was done."

"Stop right there," Sarah ordered. "First of all, I wasn't supposed to tell you about Peter's idea. So forget you heard it. Second, I thought it was dumb when Peter suggested it, and I think it's dumb now."

Heidi shook her head, sending her hair waving from side to side. "Think about it. A powerful man with a raft of bitter enemies. Did he really keel over in the middle of his coffee break? It's not impossible, but I'm not buying."

"So don't buy," said Sarah wearily. "The police aren't investigating. Even Fallon's given up. You can solve the murder on your own."

"Oh, I don't think I'd do that," said Heidi. "But you can't help but be curious."

"I can. No problem at all."

Heidi patted her on the shoulder. "I'm sorry. This has been a bad time for you. You want some advice?"

"I know I'm going to get some."

"Don't feel so guilty about feeling bad. Even privileged beauties get the blues."

"I do have a doctorate in psychology." *Oh, God,* she thought, *what a prig I am!*

But Heidi laughed. "Yeah, but you'll survive anyhow." She looked at her watch. "Eight-thirty. Come on. I'll buy the first round."

Chapter 37

The U.S. Attorney occupied several floors of a featureless structure, thrown up at the edge of Chinatown in the hope of encouraging local development. While Sarah and Heidi trailed behind, Fallon made a royal progress through the office, trading handshakes and wisecracks.

"I thought you used to work at Main Justice," whispered Sarah.

"I did. But I got around."

After the luxury of Arant and Devries, the U.S. Attorney's digs seemed slightly seedy and decidedly chaotic. Secretaries handled half a dozen telephone lines at a time. Attorneys rushed down the hall with massive trial files tucked under their arms. Papers were heaped haphazardly. Sarah began to get an insight into Fallon's working habits.

Nat Zeldin's office was roughly half the size of Sarah's, its walls papered with crayon drawings boldly signed by "Mattie Zeldin-Peretz." Zeldin himself, who looked to be in his midthirties, reminded Sarah of the ageing postdocs who had peopled the halls at the University of Chicago.

"I'll have to go next door for an extra chair," he said apologetically, returning in a moment with a seat for Heidi. "Okay, then." He grinned as they took their places. "Three against one. That gives me just a slight advantage. What can I do for you?"

"I thought we might be able to trim this last request down to reasonable proportions," said Fallon amiably.

"Come on now, Peter," Zeldin protested. "All these requests are relevant."

"I'm not so sure about that," Fallon countered. He ticked off two or three examples culled from Sarah's memo.

Zeldin removed his horn-rimmed glasses and rubbed his eyes. "So what are you going to do? Take it to the judge? She'll throw you out in thirty seconds."

"Let's not bother her yet," Fallon agreed. He pushed his hair back from his forehead. "By the way, we haven't received your response to our summary judgment motion yet."

"Ah. I was going to mention that while you we were here. We're going to need an extension."

"Really?" Fallon was sympathetic. "You'll need our consent for that."

"Not necessarily."

"Only if you want the motion to be granted."

Zeldin grinned again. Sarah found herself warming up to her adversary.

"Let's go through the list," he said. "But I'll expect the rule of reason to prevail when you file your own next set of requests."

"Never happen," Fallon replied. "We're going to get the case tossed out on summary judgment, remember?"

Zeldin laughed. "Let's begin with request number one. Documents of Norman Finkelstein. You're not going to give me trouble about that, are you?"

In fact, Fallon raised several objections before giving way. The pattern was repeated on each item till they reached the requests Sarah had marked as most egregious. Here the scenario was reversed. Zeldin aggressively rejected Fallon's objections, then grudgingly agreed to retract the requests.

In the end, the actual disagreement boiled down to a handful of documents involving computer software. After considerable wrangling, Fallon proposed a compromise: West Bank would provide edited versions omitting technical information that might be useful to business rivals.

"That ought to satisfy you, Nat. I know what you want the software documents for and these redactions won't be a problem."

Zeldin rubbed his eyes. "I'm inclined to agree just so I can get you out of my office. But I'd better get my investigator up here before I commit. He's the one who really understands the details of the software. Anyone want a cup of coffee?"

They declined. Sarah wondered if the offer conjured up thoughts of Wolfson's death in each of their minds. If so, no one let on.

A few minutes later, Zeldin returned with an athletic-looking young man who seemed to fill the small room to capacity. He seemed somehow familiar, and Sarah decided that he reminded her of a younger version of Sterling Gray. Judging from the careful scrutiny Heidi accorded the stranger, she must have noted the resemblance as well.

"Mike McCoy," said Zeldin, introducing his investigator. "Peter, could you tell Mike exactly what you propose?" Fallon and McCoy launched into an interminable discussion. Where the hell had Fallon learned so much about the software? Sarah pictured him reading rapidly through reams of abstruse notations, instantly digesting problem after problem. What a waste of a brilliant mind! Why had he given up on the classics? Sarah imagined him in one of his worn tweed jackets, pacing in front of rapt students, discoursing on the Athenian concept of selfhood.

Zeldin, who had looked on silently, finally broke in. "I could listen to you guys all day, but I have a trial coming up. I think I heard the two of you reach common ground about five minutes ago. If I'm wrong, don't correct me." He stood up, bringing the meeting to an end.

McCoy squeezed against Sarah as he moved out of the room. Looking over his shoulder, he gave her a playful smile.

"Well," she said to Heidi as they headed for the elevators, "the government may not have many investigators, but at least the ones they have are good-looking."

Heidi looked at her blankly, so Sarah repeated herself.

Heidi shrugged as if to say that she was really above such considerations. Sarah felt suitably rebuffed.

But she returned to her office to find salve for her ego. A

dozen long-stem roses in a crystal vase sat on the center of her desk. For a moment her heart sank. She had heard nothing from Sterling since New Year's and had no desire to attempt a fruitless reconciliation.

But the card was not from Sterling Gray. It read: "New Year's was a bore without you. Please don't say no again. How about dinner at the White House on Tuesday? The company isn't much but the food is always good."

The card was unsigned. Did his lovers call him Cicero? Or were there nicknames?

Chapter 38

Cicero Deauville might dine at the White House as a matter of course. But Sarah had never even seen a President in the flesh. Nor, until recently, had she even voted for a winning ticket.

So when the President took her hand and called her by name, she felt as though her heart would leap out through her new evening dress. *Thank God we don't have royalty,* she reflected. *I probably would have fainted.*

"Don't be so nervous," said Cicero Deauville, after introducing her in the space of ten minutes to a fellow senator, a woman astronaut, and the tough-guy star of last summer's film blockbuster. "You're easily the most beautiful woman in the room." Deauville, resplendent in a superbly tailored dinner jacket, squeezed her hand gently. He was obviously in his element.

"I'm certainly the only woman in the room whom no one's ever heard of."

"That makes you grist for their mill. They'll all be asking about you."

"Anyhow," said Sarah, "I'm not the most beautiful woman in the room, though I appreciate the thought. Who's that woman over there, the one with the diamond the size of a golf ball?"

"Softball, I'd say. That's Nancy Llewellyn."

Nancy Llewellyn favored her with a practiced smile that revealed a pearly set of slightly too-perfect teeth. Sizing up Sarah immediately as a creature without independent interest, she shifted her attention back to Deauville, offering well-phrased observations on several of their fellow guests, names familiar to Sarah from the pages of the *Post*'s Style section.

Snubbed, Sarah let her eyes wander around the historic room, drinking in the detail. How much history had been made on the spot where she now stood? An exchange of words, a quiet handshake, and the paths of nations were changed.

Cicero Deauville was tugging at her hand.

"Sarah, this is Dick Llewellyn."

As she smiled automatically into the deep-set eyes, Sarah felt the shock of delayed recognition. Richard Llewellyn, the former Secretary of State. And his wife, of course, was no longer Nancy Gray, but was now Nancy Llewellyn. Sarah studied the bare-shouldered, bejeweled figure with barely concealed fascination. So this was the cold-hearted bitch of Sterling Gray's matrimonial chamber of horrors. And to think that she, herself, might have been the second Mrs. Gray.

"You might have told me," Sarah said to Deauville as they drifted across the room.

"I thought you knew."

"You knew perfectly well I didn't. I might have started talking about Sterling or the firm and made an ass of myself."

"You? Never."

Sarah drew her finger slowly down the sleeve of his dinner jacket. "You know what I think? I think you were hoping some sparks might fly."

"You will persist in thinking the worst of me," Deauville teased. "But I assure you, it's quite unjustified."

At dinner, Sarah was placed between the movie star and a Brazilian diplomat. She had no experience in this sort of arrangement, where general conversation is an impossibility. The Brazilian was evidently fascinated by Nancy Llewellyn on his left. For a time, the movie star chatted with the First Lady. Sarah sipped soup in embarrassed silence. With the serving of the main course, the actor finally turned to Sarah with the look of a man worn out by unaccustomed social responsibilities.

"And who exactly are you? Somebody important? Or just

attached to someone important?" He turned on his famous smile. "Don't mean to be rude, but this isn't really my scene."

Sarah was surprised to find that the actor affected an American accent even off-screen. She had assumed he would sound like a bona fide Australian when the cameras stopped rolling. She glanced down to the far end of the table where the President was listening in apparent awe to the astronaut, who was presumably regaling him with stories of weightless space walks. Some touch of absurdity about the whole spectacle made her giggle.

"I'm a little offended you don't recognize me," she said.

The actor scrutinized her more carefully. "You're not in the business, are you? They wouldn't have put you next to me if you were. Hollywood gets parceled out. Seasons the broth."

"I've never been to Hollywood," Sarah said truthfully.

"A writer then. You're touring your new book. I saw you on the Today Show." The actor laughed. "I don't have the wildest idea who you are."

"Then I'm at an advantage." Sarah laughed. "Why are you here tonight?"

"Hell if I know. Listen, what's your name? Deauville introduced us but I've forgotten."

"Sarah Strasser."

"Strasser?" His brows knitted. "You're not the astronaut, are you? I know there's an astronaut here somewhere. But you don't look right for the part."

Sarah laughed. "Never been in outer space *or* Hollywood."

The actor sighed. "Very well then, we'll proceed methodically. Have no fear. I'll find you out."

The rest of dinner whirled by. Sarah was vaguely conscious that it might be rude to monopolize the movie star's attentions. But a movie star can bestow his attentions where he likes. Sarah wished that Heidi were there to enjoy the scene.

"It turned out to be a lovely evening," said Sarah as Deauville's limousine rolled down Pennsylvania Avenue.

"Lovely for you," grumbled Deauville. "I had the pleasure of watching you chat with a film star while that old bag from the

Arts Council put the squeeze on me. I think we need to spend a little time talking to each other."

He slid open the panel separating them from the chauffeur. "Harry, let's stop at the Willard."

"I really don't want to go out," said Sarah. "I feel like I'm in costume."

"In that case, we'll go back to my apartment."

Sarah smiled. "I don't kiss on a first date."

Deauville laughed. "Neither do I. I'm from Louisiana. We'll go back to my place and Harry will drive you home in an hour, tops. What do you say?"

Deauville's apartment at the Watergate commanded a panoramic view of the river. Sarah took a seat on a sofa upholstered in pale raw silk and gazed at the lights, while Deauville popped open a bottle of champagne and slipped on a CD. The hypnotic murmurings of a Windham Hill sampler resonated through the expensive speakers. *What a waste*, reflected Sarah, who regarded New Age productions as yuppie elevator music.

"So," said Deauville, seating himself at the opposite end of the couch. "Bring me up to date. How's the firm coping with the loss of Felix Wolfson?"

Sarah had been expecting a more intimate line of inquiry.

"We're getting over the shock."

"Are you? No lingering repercussions?"

"How do you mean?"

Deauville shrugged. "The man just about *was* Arant and Devries. He doesn't disappear like a pebble in a lake."

"Of course not. Peter Fallon is taking over a lot of his work."

"Ah, the king is dead, long live the king. I suppose they'll be pinning their hopes on Fallon now. But I wonder if his heart will really be in it?"

Sarah frowned. "No one is more intense than Peter. You should know that."

"And indeed I do." Deauville rose to refill her glass. "And what about you? I suppose Fallon is grooming you as his protégée."

Sarah laughed. "I'm a first-year associate. I'm light years from being anyone's protégée."

"But you're not just any associate. You're my lawyer."

Sarah looked at him keenly, but Deauville seemed to be counting the bubbles in his glass. "I wouldn't think you have much need of legal counsel these days," she replied.

"But I do." Deauville laughed. "And so do my friends and colleagues."

"A big case coming up?"

"Lots of big cases," said Deauville. "I'm in a position to swing a lot of business your way. Which will make you very much an attorney to be reckoned with. In the firm and around town. Beautiful, talented, and a rainmaker."

Sarah suddenly felt very tired. What was Deauville up to? Whatever it was, it would have to wait.

"I'm sorry," she said. "I don't mean to drink and run, but I'd like that ride home."

Deauville glanced at his watch. "It's not even midnight." He stood up and held out a hand. "It's my fault as usual. I'm so excited to have you here that I don't know the right thing to say. Just come and stand with me here for a few minutes."

Deauville slipped his arm around her and escorted to the broad windows.

"I love this city," he said. "It draws the most fascinating people in the world. If you love money, you up-stakes for New York. But if you go in search of power, this will be your destination."

"It doesn't sound very lovable."

Deauville gently stroked her hair. "Lovable? Not always lovable, no. But once you're under the spell, it can be a good deal more powerful than love."

Sarah felt Deauville's warm hands slide down her bare arms. Through the windows, lights reflected in the silent river below. Deauville pressed his lips against hers.

Sarah put her arms around him in weary acquiescence. To her surprise, Deauville kissed clumsily, as if his mouth lacked feeling. Sterling Gray, whatever his failings, had been sensitive and adroit in matters of this kind. After a minute, Sarah was longing for their embrace to end.

But Deauville was not similarly inclined. His hands pressed tight against the small of her back as he bent to nuzzle her neck.

Sarah pushed him away with a feigned air of playfulness.

"I told you I never kiss on a first date. It's time for me to leave before my limo turns into a pumpkin."

Deauville bent to kiss her hand, then grazed his lips along he length of her arm.

"Harry won't turn into a pumpkin. He can take you any time."

Sarah tried to pull her arm away. "Please, I'm really very tired. It's time for me to go."

Deauville's arms encircled her again. "Honey, no one is asking you to do anything. Just relax." Once more his mouth descended on hers. Sarah tried to turn aside but found herself locked in his embrace. Panic rose inside her. Reaching for the back of his head, she pulled his hair with all her strength. Deauville gave no sign of noticing, but his teeth sank hard into her lip, causing her to cry out.

As if on cue, Deauville pushed her back on to the sofa. With one hand, Deauville trapped her hands together behind her back and clenched them tight. Pinioned by her own weight, they were useless to her. Deauville's free hand moved up her dress to her thigh. His mouth nibbled at her breast through the gossamer gown.

Sarah nearly succumbed to tears of shame and horror. She tried to kick Deauville in the groin, but he had planted himself between her legs. His hand thrust upward under her dress.

In desperation, Sarah leaned forward to the Senator's offered neck and bit viciously into the flesh. With a shout of pained surprise, he moved to get out of reach. For an instant, his grip relaxed.

With greater strength than she knew she possessed, Sarah hurled herself off the couch. Deauville grabbed hold of her ankle, but she kicked loose and tumbled toward the door.

It was locked.

Sarah looked in horror at the three inscrutable locks. Deauville struggled to his feet. Droplets of blood trickled down his neck. She flipped the top lock and yanked at the door. It opened.

Sarah ran pell-mell down the softly-lighted corridor. The elevator was directly ahead. But how long would it take? Throwing open the emergency exit, she rushed down the concrete steps, nearly stumbling in her haste. As she reached the penultimate landing, pursuing footsteps echoed in the stairwell. Terrified, she threw herself over the railing and dropped the last flight, crashing to the bottom of the staircase with a cruel thud.

For a moment, she thought she had broken her knee. The pain throbbed violently. *It's just a bruise,* she said to herself. *It's nothing.* She pushed open the heavy steel door and stepped from the concrete stairwell into the thickly carpeted lobby.

Outside, Harry the chauffeur was killing time with the doorman. While their backs were turned, she rushed down the entrance ramp to Virginia Avenue.

The wind off the river blew through her thin dress. It could have been an arctic blizzard and Sarah would not have cared. Her anger would have burned it away.

Chapter 39

Fallon had begun dreaming of Forrest Labs. He woke at night from tormented visions of recondite medical debates with imaginary witnesses. Minutes would pass before he could determine whether he had chanced on a brilliant new argument. Invariably, he had not.

There was nothing new about this pattern. When Fallon was married, Alexis would brew a pot of tea and they would take turns reading aloud. When sleep was particularly elusive, Fallon would recite half-forgotten passages from Euripides. This extreme remedy was sufficient for all but the toughest cases of insomnia.

Now that he was living alone, it was a relief to return to the office with first light. Soon Jeff Unruh would expect to see him at Forrest Labs headquarters in New Jersey. And this time the hard-drinking CEO would want to hear his plan of action.

Fallon had just sent another sheaf of document summaries back to the file room when Sarah Strasser stepped into the office.

"What on earth happened to you?" Her right knee was bound by a thick ace bandage. As he moved to pull up a chair, he noticed an ugly cut on her lip and a bruise under her left eye.

"Is it okay if we shut the door?" she asked.

She was evidently making a great effort to appear controlled. For a moment she sat wordlessly.

"Was it an accident?" Fallon prompted finally, sure that it was not.

Sarah managed a strained smile. "It's funny. All last night I thought about coming in to talk to you. I rehearsed quite elaborately." She paused, as if gathering her energies. "I went out with Cicero Deauville last night."

Fallon's heart sank. It was almost as if he had seen it coming.

"Dinner at the White House. Then back to his apartment for champagne. Promises of power and glory when I became his lawyer-lover. I guess he figured I'd just fall into bed. When I didn't, he tried to rape me."

"He tried—"

"He didn't succeed. I banged the knee getting away. It's not as bad as it looks."

Fallon got to his feet and paced over to the window, hands thrust deep in his pockets. He could feel Sarah's eyes following him. His initial relief gave way to a tide of anger. Anger at Deauville. Disgust with himself, the Senator's hired gun.

"We knew it all the time, didn't we?" said Sarah. "Deep down."

"I tried to believe he was innocent," said Fallon. "But you're right. I blinded myself."

"I was worse than you," said Sarah. "You just did your job. I went up to his apartment, let him kiss me. I'm sure some people would say I got what was coming."

"Only a moral imbecile."

Unconsciously, Sarah ran a finger over the cut on her lip. "Is there anything we can do?"

Fallon dropped back into a chair. "That's up to you, of course. We can bring an assault charge against Deauville."

Sarah shook her head. "I know I should. But I don't think I could stand it."

"I don't blame you. It would be virtually impossible to prove. I doubt we could get the prosecutor interested. And it would be hell for you."

"What I really meant," said Sarah, "is whether there's anything we can do about the Andrea Callas trial? I mean, we know now that Deauville must have been guilty."

"Andrea Callas knew Deauville was guilty. She knew it when I cross-examined her." Fallon recalled the dark eyes gazing into his own as he led her step by step away from the truth. "And Irene Shaughnessy knew he was guilty. But we made sure she didn't speak."

Painfully, Sarah got to her feet. "So that's it. We did our job and now we have to live with it. Right?" She limped to the door.

But living with it wouldn't be easy, Fallon reflected as he helped Molly with her homework that evening. Alexis was off at the Hellenic Society. Molly seized the opportunity to have her father do her math assignment.

"Come on now," said Fallon. "I said I'd help. You won't learn anything if I do it for you."

"I'll see how it's supposed to be done," said Molly innocently.

"Don't be clever. You do the next problem yourself and then I'll go over it with you."

Molly bit the end of her pencil intently. Fallon sat back to watch her cogitate. You wanted your kid to be proud of you. What would Molly think if she knew the truth about Cicero Deauville? No need to ask. A nine-year-old could be devastatingly clear-sighted.

"I'm stuck," she said.

Fallon grinned. "You haven't had time to get stuck." He checked his watch. "You finish up and I'll get dinner ready."

Fallon slipped a tray of moussaka into the microwave and set the table. There would be time to give Sarah a call before dinner. Fallon picked up the phone, then hesitated. What Sarah really needed was to talk to another woman. He dialed Heidi Hollings's number at work, but got her voice mail. Fallon left a message. It was only a quarter to seven. She might still be around.

"Nice cooking, Dad," said Molly wryly as she dug in. "What do you eat when you're home? I mean, when you don't order in from the Hunan Garden?"

"Domino's pizza," said Fallon promptly.

"Daddy! When you actually cook at home."

"Frozen dinners."

"Is that all you know how to cook?"

"Who cooks them? I suck them frozen."

Molly rolled her eyes. "We saw that movie together at the Biograph. That's a Woody Allen joke."

"You're too smart for your own good," said Fallon. "Just for that, tonight I'm going to beat you at chess."

But he let her win after all, though he made it convincingly difficult. In two or three more years, Fallon thought, he would be hard pressed to hold his own with his little prodigy.

"You'd better get to bed," said Fallon as they put away the board. "It's already past your bedtime. If your mother finds you up, she'll kill me."

"Oh, I don't think she'll be home too early. She'll probably go out with that guy again after the meeting."

Fallon froze. "What guy?"

Molly's confusion was transparent. She knew she had said too much. But she had no guile.

"She has a new friend," Molly said reluctantly. "Sometimes they go out for a cup of coffee or something."

Or what? Fallon wanted to ask. What's his name? Does he come to the house? But he couldn't put his daughter in an impossible situation. He smiled. "Knowing your mother, she'll realize that you're not in bed and come back specially to catch you."

Molly giggled, relieved to see the tension pass. "I'll get ready. Are you going to read to me?"

"Are you kidding? I've been waiting for this all day."

When the chapter was finished and the lights were turned off, Fallon went downstairs to tidy up. Alexis should already be home. She must have stopped somewhere after the meeting. Which didn't necessarily entail romance, Fallon assured himself. People often went out for drinks after the meetings. And this new friend might be just a friend.

Fallon was unconvinced by his own soothing patter. He couldn't sit still. His stomach was in turmoil. He paced his ex-wife's living room like a lovesick adolescent.

The phone rang. Fallon grabbed it.

"Peter, is that you?" But it wasn't Alexis. It was Kara Melnik from forensics.

"Can you come on down?"

"Not yet. I'm looking after Molly. Can it keep till tomorrow?"

"Peter, listen. This is business. We've got a body down here. A young woman. No ID. But she has a card-key for your office building. I thought you might be able to identify her."

Fallon thought he might be sick. So Deauville had killed her. The bastard must have panicked. Fallon stared numbly at the phone. A key turned in the lock.

Chapter 40

Fallon followed Kara Melnik across the brightly lit room. The neon lights, tiled walls, and stainless-steel trolleys always reminded him of the cafeteria kitchen in Adams House, where he had bussed trays for more hours than he cared to remember. But the trolley in front of him now didn't carry plates and silverware. A foot protruded from under the sheet. A gray tag hung from the toe.

"For God's sake, Fallon. You look green. Have you gone soft at your law firm?"

"Let's see her."

Kara pulled back the sheet. "Shot in the chest at very close range. Matter of inches. A .38. Nothing special there."

The pale-blond hair was still pulled into a knot. Fallon gazed at the thin, surprisingly muscular arms. The fun and mischief had fled from the glassy eyes. The spark was out.

"Her name is Heidi Hollings," said Fallon. "She's a lawyer at the firm."

"A friend?"

"She was becoming a friend."

Kara pulled up the sheet. "I'm sorry."

"Where was she found?" Fallon asked as they returned to Kara's office.

"In the woods by the P Street beach." This was a grassy area at the edge of Rock Creek Park, a few blocks from Dupont Circle. In the summer months it was thick with sunbathers. "She was wearing a jogging suit. Must have been coming out of the park at the end of a run." Kara shook her head sadly. "These young girls think they're immortal. Running in Rock Creek Park after dark is courting death."

"When did it happen?"

"Someone heard the gunshot and actually called the police. Believe it or not. A glimmer of civic responsibility. The call came in at eight twenty-eight.

"I figured she was a secretary," Kara continued. "She didn't look old enough to be a lawyer. Poor kid."

"You wouldn't have thought she was a lawyer if you had met her," said Fallon. "She was so unpredictable, so full of life."

"This is a hard town."

"Too hard." He felt very weary. He looked for a place to sit, but the single chair was occupied by a box of files. "Some days I wonder how my heart doesn't break."

Kara studied him through her circular wire rims. "Let's grab a cup of coffee."

"It's after midnight. I'd better go home."

Kara shook her head. "I'm wise to you, Fallon. You're going back to that big empty apartment and brood." She slipped her arm through his and headed for the door.

"Where are we going?"

"Georgetown Cafe. First-class milkshakes twenty-four hours a day." She pulled her coat from the rack. "You're buying, moneybags."

Chapter 41

At three the next afternoon, Sarah walked into his office with an air of detached calm. Fallon had broken the news to her in the morning after an excruciating phone call to Heidi's parents. It had been an agonizing day.

"Did the super give you the key to Heidi's apartment?"

Fallon nodded.

"I just remembered Heidi's cat. We can't leave him in there." Fallon stood up and retrieved his tweed coat from the closet.

"I can go alone," said Sarah.

"Some fresh air will do me good."

The afternoon was damp and raw as they walked slowly across Dupont Circle. "I suppose you can give the cat to the pound," Fallon suggested. "Or you could put up a notice at the firm."

"I'm adopting him," said Sarah shortly.

"Ah."

A minute later, Sarah said, "Heidi was going to move back to Nebraska, you know. She was going to do something she enjoyed, be with people she trusted."

They hurried across Q Street as the lights changed.

"Is the leg okay?" asked Fallon.

"Hurts like hell. But the doctor said it's good to walk on it."

A couple of blocks east of the circle, the upscale gentrification started to peter out. Many of the beautiful old brownstones were slipping into irreparable disrepair. The corner of 15th and R was only a ten-minute walk from the firm; but it was a world away.

"I told her it was crazy to live over here," said Sarah. "But Heidi said she wouldn't double her rent to live three blocks farther west. I wish that for once she had taken my advice."

"Well, it wouldn't have made any difference," said Fallon.

"Except that she'd be alive now."

"If Heidi was going to jog at night in Rock Creek Park, it didn't much matter where she lived."

Sarah stopped short. "Heidi was killed in Rock Creek Park?"

"By the P Street beach."

Sarah shook her head. "Wait a moment. That makes no sense at all. Heidi never ran in the park. She jogged the same route every day. Up Connecticut as far as the Hilton, then over to her apartment to feed the cat. Then back to the firm. I'd run it with her sometimes."

"I can't help it," said Fallon. "She was killed in the park."

Heidi's apartment was a third-floor walk-up. The hall was musty and unpromising. But when they stepped inside, Fallon understoods Heidi's refusal to move. He would have done the same. The space had been transformed into a single enormous room with a sleep loft. Even on a cloudy afternoon, the light poured in through several skylights. Heidi had hung the white walls with country quilts. Colorful rag rugs were scattered about on the highly polished floor. There was almost no furniture. A gray-and-white cat rubbed its head against Sarah's leg.

She bent down to pick it up. "Hi there, Popcorn." She turned to Fallon. "See? He remembers me."

Sarah put out some food and water. "He's ravenous. And there are no empty cans of cat food in the trash. I'll bet he hasn't eaten since yesterday morning."

"She must have changed her jogging route," said Fallon. "And she never made it home."

"I don't believe it," Sarah declared. "Heidi took risks. But not pointless risks. Why the hell would she suddenly want to run in the park on a freezing winter evening? Do they know when she was shot?"

"Someone called in the gunshot at about eight-thirty."

"Heidi always began her run before seven so that there would still be people on the streets."

"I tried to call her around six-forty-five," Fallon remembered. "No answer."

"So she was already gone by then. Her whole run didn't take more than forty minutes, plus the time in her apartment. Say an hour total at the absolute most." Sarah sat down in an antique rocking chair, grimacing as she stretched her leg.

"Suppose you're right and Heidi didn't jog in the park," said Fallon. "In that case, someone put her body in the park and called the police." He looked at Sarah sharply. "A pretty elaborate script. Do you know something that I don't?"

Sarah blushed. "I told Heidi your idea that Wolfson's coffee had been poisoned. It turned out she had been thinking along the same lines."

Fallon dropped onto a spindly settee. "So you think Heidi played Nancy Drew and went in search of the murderer?"

"What do you think? You knew Heidi."

Fallon dug his hands into his coat pockets. Could it be true? Had Heidi's extraordinary mind solved the mystery of Wolfson's murder? Would she have been brash enough to confront the killer?

Fallon pictured Heidi getting into Devries' Jaguar for a tête-à-tête. But Devries couldn't have killed Heidi. There was no way he could have moved body to the park. On the other hand, Charlotte could have managed. And it would have been child's play for Ken Bradley.

"Would you say that Cicero Deauville was capable of murder?" Fallon mused.

"Cicero Deauville? I'm the wrong person to ask. If you can think of a motive, I'm ready to convict him."

"I can't think of a reason in the world why he would kill Heidi. Or Wolfson for that matter." Fallon shrugged. "On the other hand, he's violent, ruthless, and clever. That probably counts for something."

It was beginning to get dark. In a storefront across the street a neon sign advertised check cashing and money orders.

Sarah struggled to her feet. "I'm going to find something to carry Popcorn in."

Sarah searched a walk-in closet, emerging with a large wicker basket. With surprisingly little effort, she persuaded Popcorn to jump in.

"So what now?" she asked. "Wait for the killer to make a mistake and reveal himself?"

"That could be very dangerous," said Fallon. "I have a better idea."

Chapter 42

"Hi. This is Maurice Politz. I'll be on vacation till February 8. Please leave a message at the tone. If you need help immediately, please accept my referral to the Lester Magnuson agency."

"So it's pronounced 'pole-eats' " Fallon observed. "I wonder if that's a Cajun name?"

Lester Magnuson was unavailable. But his secretary proved obliging. Mr. Politz was on vacation. He was down in the bayous doing some serious bass fishing. No, she wasn't supposed to give out his number. Well, if he was Mr. Politz's lawyer. If it was really urgent . . .

"You ever been to New Orleans?" said Fallon when he hung up.

Popcorn had fallen asleep in Sarah's lap. She softly stroked the fluffy fur.

"Only to change planes."

"How about a new experience?"

"I don't get it," said Sarah. "What do you think this Politz is going to tell you?"

"If I knew, I wouldn't need to fly across the country to ask him." Fallon ran his hands through his hair. "Why start with Politz? Mostly because I don't know where else to begin."

"That's reassuring."

Fallon grinned. "It's not just a whim for Creole cooking. Look,

159

I'm assuming that Wolfson had the Deauville files in his office for a reason—with Wolfson, there was a reason for everything. He had annotated Politz's expense report with question marks. Maybe that means something, maybe it doesn't." Fallon paused. "And there's a link to Heidi. She was curious about the private investigator also. Remember her remarks at your Christmas dinner with Ken Bradley? That's what made us look into Wolfson's files in the first place."

"I suppose it's worth a shot," Sarah conceded. "But what about Popcorn? I can't leave him alone in his new home."

"My daughter will take care of him. It's only for one night. Two at the most."

Sarah struggled to her feet. "It'll be more fun than working on West Bank anyway."

"One thing," said Fallon. "I want you to humor me. Take a cab home. Don't let anyone in. And I mean, anyone."

"What if I get hungry?"

"Starve. I promise you a good dinner tomorrow."

Fallon had hoped to talk to Ken Bradley alone. But he found him huddled over a deposition transcript with Sterling Gray. It was just seven o'clock. Where had Bradley been twenty-four hours earlier?

For half an hour, the three lawyers discussed strategy in Forrest Labs. Finally, Fallon got up and stretched. "Guess I'll walk home." He shook his head. "After last night, I won't be able to pass the entrance to the park without thinking of Heidi."

Gray nodded sadly. "I was thinking the same thing myself earlier. By the way, I did everything you asked me to. Heidi's parents will be flying in tomorrow to pick up the body. All the arrangements are made."

Bradley said nothing. For weeks—ever since Wolfson's death—his old easy warmth had disappeared.

"Do you guys ever get out of here before ten?" Fallon asked.

"I don't see you running out early," Bradley replied curtly. "Do you expect me to do less?"

"Of course not. But even I spend the evening with Molly once in a while. Last night, for example."

"Unfortunately, that wasn't an early night for the worker bees," said Gray.

"No break for dinner?"

"Ken ordered in from Red Sage."

"I have to lay off those chilpotle peppers," said Bradley.

"We didn't eat till eight-thirty," said Gray, "and I didn't get home till midnight."

"Later for me," Bradley added.

"You make me feel guilty," said Fallon. "I'll get back to work."

Dinner at eight-thirty. A perfect alibi for a murder phoned in at eight-twenty-eight. But Bradley could easily have picked up Heidi in his car as she set off on her run at a quarter to seven. It wouldn't have taken him more than fifteen minutes to dispose of the body. Back at the firm, he could call the police at his leisure.

Fallon stopped in his office for his coat. At the far end of the hall, the lights burned in Devries' office. Since Wolfson's death, St. John was once more savoring the delights of unchallenged premiership. He wined and dined clients and worked till all hours. But between seven and eight last night, so far as Fallon could ascertain, his whereabouts were unknown.

Fallon walked the few blocks over to the park and looked down at the P Street Beach. It looked distinctly uninviting this time of night. Still, thought Fallon, Heidi could easily have taken a detour this way. In which case her death was just another of the capital's pointless daily tragedies.

Instead of turning toward Foggy Bottom and home, Fallon crossed P Street and headed for the genial opulence of the Ritz. Charlotte Devries had arrived early. He joined her in the bar, where she sat nursing a Dubonnet at a secluded table. Fallon ordered a ginger ale.

"We have to stop meeting like this, Peter. People will talk." Charlotte smiled into his eyes and cupped one of his hands in hers.

"People know better than that," said Fallon lightly.

"Why should they? An attractive woman seen drinking with a most attractive man. Should they really know better?"

Fallon steeled himself against the siren's song like Ulysses

Mark Stern

strapped to the mast of his ship. "I'm afraid we have to talk business."

"Oh, dear." Charlotte's wide mouth turned down. "How dreary."

"Why did you lie to me?" Fallon asked. "St. John knew about your affair and the photograph. He was trying to get it back from Wolfson an hour before he died."

Charlotte freed his captive hand and took a sip of Dubonnet. She gave no indication of surprise. "Now, Peter, let me ask you— why should I have told you the truth?"

"I prefer to ask why you would lie. Did you suspect that St. John had killed Wolfson? Were you trying to protect him?"

"You won't think me stupid, will you, Peter, but why should I think *anyone* killed Felix? He died of a heart attack."

"The idea of poison might have crossed your mind."

"It might, but it didn't." Charlotte opened her pocketbook and drew out a packet of Rothmans. "You don't mind if I have a cigarette, do you? St. John forbids them absolutely."

She drew the smoke deep into her lungs and breathed out gracefully in the fashion of years gone by.

"I'm afraid I'm addicted to the old-fashioned vices." She smiled. "Is this just friendly probing or are you pursuing some sort of investigation? Once a prosecutor always a prosecutor?"

"I'm trying to find out why you were dishonest with me."

"Oh, dear." Charlotte's eyes were laughing at him. "How did you discover my little white lie?"

Fallon felt a slight shudder run down his spine. This woman would be capable of anything, he thought. She just didn't give a damn.

"Where were you last night between seven and eight?"

"Really, Peter. Now we're reaching new lows. Are you going to tell me the crime and read me my rights?"

"You don't have to tell me if you prefer not to."

Charlotte smiled. "It's no secret. I was at home reading."

"By yourself?"

"Did you think I had already taken another lover?"

Fallon had enough. He raised a hand for the check.

"I haven't annoyed you, have I, Peter? But you really can't

expect me to answer these questions with a straight face. If you want a drink, call me any time. But leave these silly antics to the police."

But Charlotte knew better than that, Fallon reflected as he stepped outside. Battling an epidemic of murder, the D.C. police had neither the resources nor the inclination to pursue a lawyer's speculations about poisoned coffee and jogging routes. There were a lot of advantages to living in the murder capital of the country—if you wanted to get away with murder.

Chapter 43

"You're quite a salesman, Mr. Fallon," Sarah grumbled. "'Come with me to New Orleans!' I don't believe we're going to New Orleans at all. And what about the great food? A catfish sandwich at a roadside diner?"

She gazed out at the dreary winter landscape as the car turned onto yet another featureless road.

Fallon grinned. "Oh, I don't know. The Atchafalaya Basin Swamp is almost New Orleans. And what was the matter with lunch? I thought catfish is supposed to be trendy?" He consulted the map in his right hand, gripping the steering wheel with his left. "One nice thing about the South is that you can always get a Dr Pepper. Maybe I should move down here."

"You'd fit right in—the classic good ole boy."

"You laugh," said Fallon, "but there are hidden depths to my character."

"Sure. I can see you now at the general store discussing Aristotle with Billie Bob, Jethro, and the rest of the gang."

"Snob."

The car pulled into a rutted gravel driveway. A weedy front lawn stretched back to a tiny shotgun-style house. A rusting outboard motor sat square in the middle of the grass like a forlorn sculpture. A gray-haired man wearing a netted cap was rummaging in the rear of a battered pickup truck. An enormous belly

164

pushed against the frayed lumberjack shirt. Fallon bounded out of the car.

"Mr. Politz?"

"Who is it who's asking?" At least Sarah was fairly sure that this was his greeting. The thick Cajun accent left open interesting possibilities.

"Peter Fallon. From Arant and Devries." Fallon stuck out a hand. The man ignored it. He seemed to be having his own problems deciphering Fallon's Boston accent.

Despite the chilly reception, Fallon seemed perfectly at ease. "You are Mr. Politz, aren't you?"

"What's it to you?"

Fallon grinned. "I think I see the problem. I'm looking for *Maurice* Politz. Is he around?"

The man stared ahead phlegmatically.

"No problem," said Fallon. "I can always mail the check. Just thought I'd drop by, seeing as how I was in the area."

"What check?" The brown eyes shifted from Fallon to Sarah and back again.

"It's only fifteen hundred dollars. Payment left over from the last job. But it can wait." Fallon turned back to the car.

"Hold on. You can leave the check with me."

Fallon shook his head. "I couldn't do that. Can't leave the money with a stranger."

"I'm no stranger. I'm his dad."

"Yeah, I figured that," said Fallon. "But rules are rules. I'll have bookkeeping issue a new check when I get back to Washington. It'll take a while, but it'll get there."

"Why, hell!" The senior Politz was incensed. "Are you some Washington bureaucrat? Maurice ain't but forty-five miles away. He's fishing at the bayou. He'll be back tonight."

Fallon ran a hand through his hair, which somehow managed to look even more tousled than usual. Though down here, Sarah reflected, he was the height of fashion.

"I'll tell you what," said Fallon. "I've got some business to discuss with Maurice. If you tell me how to find him, I'll drive over right now."

The man snorted. "You'll never find it on your own." He threw open the door to his pickup. "Just follow me."

"He'll drive forty-five miles to make sure you deliver the check today?" said Sarah wonderingly as they headed back down the highway.

"I told you you were a snob."

"Well, I was wrong about you. You'd make a great good ole boy. We just have to get you one of those caps."

"I've got an old Red Sox cap at home. We'll see if I pass muster."

After an hour, just as Sarah began to suspect a wild-goose chase, they plunged into the swamp. Five minutes later, the paved road ended. Following close behind the pickup, they bounced their way down an overgrown trail.

"Where in God's name are we?" Sarah asked. "This reminds me of the Everglades."

Fallon laughed. "It must have been a pretty sedate corner of the Everglades. This is just the edge of the swamp. We can't be all that far from the metropolis of Whisky River Landing." He pointed ahead. "I think I spy water. And with luck, the gentleman standing by the truck will be Maurice."

Maurice might have been a snapshot of his father twenty years earlier. The hairline was lower, the belly less fully established. Otherwise, there wasn't a lot to choose between them.

As the strangers advanced, Maurice placed a last fishing rod in the rack on the front of his pickup.

"This fellah has money for you," his father announced when they were still twenty steps away. "Fifteen hundred."

Maurice did not seem pleased by the glad tidings. His eyes narrowed. "Who the hell are you?"

"Peter Fallon from Arant and Devries."

Once again, Fallon's outstretched hand was ignored. "What do you want?"

"I don't want anything. Our bookkeeper found we still owed you fifteen hundred dollars. I was down this way on business and thought I'd drop by in person to tender my thanks. We owe a lot to you."

Politz silently opened the cab of his truck. When he turned around, he was wielding a shotgun.

"Now suppose you just tell me what you really want?"

"Maurice," his father demanded. "What the fuck is happening?"

"Shut up." Maurice nodded at Fallon. "What the hell are you up to?"

Jesus Christ, thought Sarah. *This fifth-generation inbred maniac will kill us and feed us to the alligators. And no one will ever have the slightest clue what happened to us.* She imagined their car sinking slowly into the murky waters of the swamp.

Fallon laughed. "I've never seen a man so put off by good news." Reaching slowly into the breast pocket of his tweed jacket, he pulled out an envelope.

"Fifteen hundred dollars. On the account of Arant and Devries. Open it up."

Maurice inspected the check. Although his expression remained unchanged, the gun shifted toward the ground.

"What's this for?"

"I told you. Bookkeeping error. You were supposed to get a bonus when we won the case. God knows you deserve it. I'd have been sunk without you."

"You worked on the Deauville case?"

Fallon grinned. "And I thought I was famous. Sure. I did the trial."

Maurice leaned back against the truck. He pulled out a packet of Red Man chewing tobacco and stuck a wad in his cheek. "Well, I guess that's all right then."

"Well, what did I tell you?" his father snapped. "There was no call for you to speak to me disrespectful."

"Who's the lady?" Maurice asked.

"Sarah Strasser. Another lawyer on the case."

Maurice winked at Fallon. "That's real nice," he said slyly. "If there's nothing else, I'll be getting on home."

"Just one thing," said Fallon. "Help me out on this. How did you ever discover about Irene Shaughnessy and the sanatorium? That was brilliant work."

Maurice stiffened. "I thought you were Senator Deauville's lawyer?"

"You're damn right I am," said Fallon.

Maurice shot a stream of tobacco juice into the dirt. "Then ask Deauville."

He hoisted himself into the pickup and started the motor. His father was already clambering into his own truck. A minute later, Sarah was left alone with Fallon in the fading light.

"When did you get to be so cool?" she asked.

Fallon laughed. "Don't tell me you get scared just because a crooked P.I. pulls a gun in a deserted swamp? Didn't you learn anything in law school?"

Chapter 44

It was dark when they arrived at the Dauphine Orleans, a small hostelry on a quiet street of the French Quarter. For an hour they walked down the crowded byways of the town, past the toney galleries of Royale Street and the bawdy strip joints on Bourbon, where barkers were already opening doors to offer tourists a peek at the merchandise. Sidewalk stands sold twenty-four-ounce beers and "hurricanes," a local brain twister. A discordant blend of Dixieland, country western, and rock wafted down the street, together with a more harmonious blend of Cajun cooking smells.

"They're already getting ready for Mardi Gras," Fallon observed.

"Now that would be worth seeing."

"I came down for Mardi Gras my first year of college. Eight of us in a VW minivan. It was right after *Easy Rider* came out. Dennis Hopper blew his mind in New Orleans." Fallon chuckled reminiscently. "So did we."

Sarah tried to picture Fallon as a stoned-out Harvard hippie. The whole concept seemed like an oxymoron.

"Did you have hair down to your waist?"

Fallon laughed. "It's embarrassing even to think about it. Looking back, I'm amazed we didn't get into any trouble on the trip down. That was before the days of the New South."

169

"You know," said Sarah, "you're only ten years older than me, but I feel like I was born into a different world." They passed by the romantic frontage of Antoine's. "Why don't we eat here?" Sarah suggested. "Or do you want to be trendy and go to Chef K-Paul's? You decide."

"I've got a little place in mind."

"I'm starved."

"Let's get the car."

Sarah was exasperated. "Peter. We're in New Orleans. Why on earth can't we eat in the Quarter?"

"Because you said I could choose."

Twenty minutes later, they were on the outskirts of the city in a uniquely unpicturesque part of town. Fallon pulled up beside a restaurant that might have been the twin of their lunchtime roadhouse.

"Is this a joke?" Sarah demanded.

"It's Mosca's," said Fallon. "And better palates than mine claim it's the best place in town."

At their table, Fallon drank a Dr Pepper as they waited for the food to arrive. "We'll share," he said. "The baked oysters Mosca can't be missed. The barbecued shrimp is a knockout. I don't want to deprive myself of either."

Sarah took a sip of white wine, identified by her waitress as a "suave." "So what do you make of Maurice?" she asked. "I thought he might drop us in the swamp and bury the car."

Fallon laughed. "I can see it now. Remember the end of *Psycho*, when they haul the car out of the swamp?" He motioned for another Dr Pepper. "I don't think Maurice is a murderer. He's just scared, and he couldn't figure us out."

"What does he have to be scared of?"

"That's what we have to find out," said Fallon. "But I'll give you one brilliant deduction—Maurice is no hot-shot investigator. That man has trouble staying one step ahead of a bass."

"So what did he mean when he said we should ask Deauville about Irene Shaughnessy?"

"Intriguing, isn't it? Was Maurice just telling us to get lost? Or did he have something in mind?"

The waitress set down enormous plates of food. Without ceremony, Sarah dug into the oysters.

"I apologize," she said a few minutes later. "I shouldn't have
doubted you. The food is out of this world."

"Try the shrimp. But save room for the bread pudding."

When the waitress brought coffee, Sarah leaned back content-
edly. "I'm sorry we fly back tomorrow morning. I could stand a
few more meals like this."

"Actually," said Fallon, "I've planned a small detour. I thought
we might drive to the little town of Magnolia and make a stop
at the Oak Knoll sanitarium."

"Are you going to tell me why? Or will it be a surprise?"

"Surprise."

They started out early the next morning. Fallon insisted on
stopping at the Cafe Du Monde for coffee and beignets before
hitting the road.

"I feel guilty that we didn't get to spend time in town," he
explained. "Maybe we'll come back some time just for fun."

"Let's do it," Sarah replied, and only later did it occur to her
that it was an odd invitation, coming from Fallon.

She was silent as they crossed the long causeway across Lake
Ponchartrain and traveled north. For the hundredth time, she
reviewed their short list of suspects.

"Listen," said Sarah, "I'd love to convict Deauville of murder.
But the killer had to be someone at the firm. He had to put the
poison in Wolfson's coffee to begin with. Then, after the murder,
he had to remove the bag of Barrister Blend to dispose of the
evidence."

"The entire firm emptied out after you discovered Wolfson's
body," said Fallon. "Anyone could have gone back into Wolfson's
office that afternoon."

"So how could Deauville insert the poison into the coffee in
the first place?"

"Deauville was at the firm often enough," said Fallon. "Besides, he had a card key. We gave it to him during the trial."

After an hour, they left the interstate for the back roads. At a dilapidated shack, Fallon stopped for a Dr Pepper and some directions.

"That place might have come out of *Tobacco Road,*" said Sarah as they pulled back on to the road. "Where's all the antebellum splendor?"

"Not much left. The aristocracy these days build their nouveau riche castles around the golf courses."

In twenty minutes, they entered Magnolia. Four blocks later, they were driving out of town.

"We passed a sign for Oak Knoll," Sarah complained, "but you went by so quickly I couldn't read it."

Fallon grinned. "Aren't car trips fun? On the way back, I'll let you read the map. We'll never be on speaking terms again."

"There's another sign. At least we're going in the right direction."

"Look at that," said Fallon as they rounded a curve. "There's a bit of antebellum splendor after all."

Set back from the road in its own lush parkland, Oak Knoll was a rambling two-story mansion. Scarlett O'Hara would have been at home in a hammock on the broad veranda. Only when they reached the end of the drive did they spot a second, more recent building hidden by a grove of live oaks draped in Spanish moss.

"I guess Irene Shaughnessy wasn't exactly destitute," said Sarah, surveying the grounds.

"No," said Fallon thoughtfully. "This must be the place where Louisiana's aristocracy comes to dry out."

A uniformed employee escorted them inside. In the lobby, antique rockers were grouped cozily. Despite the season, fresh flowers had been set out in abundance.

A young woman with platinum-blond hair approached them with a bright smile of welcome.

"It's a pleasure to see you this morning."

"I'm here to see Dr. Bounpane."

"Do you have an appointment?"

"It will only take a minute." said Fallon.

"The doctor may be seeing patients."

"We can take a stroll around the grounds."

"Oh, he might be hours," the young woman exclaimed. "Just sit down and make yourselves comfortable and I'll go check."

Five minutes later, a middle-aged woman in a well-tailored suit introduced herself as Lynn Craddock. Fallon repeated his request.

"Are you looking to place a friend or family member?"

"I am."

"I'm sorry. Dr. Bounpane is fully booked today. But Dr. Alt-weiler can see you in half an hour."

Sarah glanced at Fallon. It seemed that their detour had been pointless.

"It's very confidential," Fallon explained.

"I'm sorry. You should have called before coming all this way."

Fallon leaned forward confidentially. "Senator Deauville told me I should deal exclusively with Dr. Bounpane."

Sarah was taken off guard. So was Lynn Craddock.

"Are you a friend of Senator Deauville's?"

"His friend and his lawyer." Fallon handed her his card. "Maybe you could give this to Dr. Bounpane. I won't take up more than a few minutes of his time."

"What was that about?" Sarah whispered when Craddock was gone.

"Just a hunch," said Fallon.

He had barely finished speaking when Lynn Craddock re-turned. "I caught Dr. Bounpane just as he was setting out on his rounds. He can give you a few minutes right now."

Chapter 45

They followed Craddock up a sweeping staircase. Dr. Bounpane was a kindly-looking man in his early fifties. He wore a dark
gray suit and old-fashioned tortoiseshell glasses. "Please have a
seat." It was the rich, formal accent of the deep South. "How
can I help you?"

"We represented Senator Deauville in the trial last fall," said
Fallon. "Do you remember signing an affidavit?"

Bounpane smiled. "I assume you haven't come to verify my
existence at this late date."

Fallon smiled back. "I've taken your existence on faith. But
now I need a little bit more information."

"I see." Dr. Bounpane rubbed his chin. "Do either of you
mind if I light my pipe?"

"Go right ahead," said Sarah.

"Am I to assume that you are here on behalf of Senator Deauville?" asked Dr. Bounpane, tamping down the tobacco.

Sarah glanced at Fallon. How far was he willing to go?

Fallon shook his head. "We're here on our own behalf. But my
question is very simple. You received visits from two different investigators last summer. Each one came to inquire about Irene Shaughnessy. One of them was Maurice Politz. Who was the other one?"

Dr. Bounpane blew a neat ring of smoke and watched it slowly
dissolve as it floated toward the ceiling.

"You've come a long way to ask a simple question. I assume that the answer is not without significance." He raised his eyebrows quizzically.

"If you've pledged yourself to secrecy," said Fallon, "I've come a long way for nothing. But if you're free to tell me, you have my word that the information will only be used in the interests of justice."

"The interests of justice? That's rather a flexible concept, isn't it?"

"Is it?" Fallon replied. "Irene Shaughnessy was your patient. What would justice require in her case?"

Dr. Bounpane's pipe had gone out. He lighted another match.

Sarah was mystified. Fallon sat back in his chair, the picture of relaxation.

Dr. Bounpane finally got his pipe going to his satisfaction. He sighed. "Is there ever justice for a victim? The harm they've suffered can never be undone."

"Perhaps not," said Fallon. "But Irene Shaughnessy was your responsibility. Don't you think she deserves to be vindicated?"

Another ring of smoke drifted upward. In the hall, a grandfather clock struck the quarter hour.

Dr. Bounpane seemed to make up his mind. "You mention Mr. Politz. Of course, he did come to see me."

"But not till mid-September."

"I don't have my calendar for last year," said Dr. Bounpane, "but I was on vacation for the month of August. Mr. Politz visited some time after my return."

"But another investigator saw you before Politz, didn't he?"

Bounpane nodded. "It was the day before I left on my holiday. The last day of July."

Fallon said nothing, waiting for Dr. Bounpane to go on.

"Mr. McCoy came in the morning. Unlike yourself, he had phoned for an appointment."

Sarah tried to remember why the name McCoy was so familiar. Fallon said, "Mike McCoy has the advantage of working for the government. That opens doors."

Sarah's mind whirled. The crowded room at the U.S. Attorney's office. The meeting on the West Bank documents. The government's investigator, the athletic young man who debated the fine points of computer software with Fallon.

"A government credential may open doors," said Dr. Bounpane, "but I protect the privacy of my patients from all prying eyes."

"That may be," said Fallon, "but you told McCoy that Miss Shaughnessy had released herself against your advice."

"It's a matter of record," said Dr. Bounpane defensively. "As you no doubt appreciate, we must protect ourselves against lawsuits."

"Did McCoy ask you to sign an affidavit like the one you later signed for Politz?"

"No. He just asked me for the date of Irene's release."

"I suppose McCoy explained the nature of his errand?" Fallon pressed.

Dr. Bounpane nodded. "I was saddened and confused."

"I'm sure you were. It must have been a bad shock to learn that your patient had been raped by your senator." Fallon leaned forward. "But that didn't stop you from calling Deauville, did it? When Mike McCoy drove out of town, you got on the phone to Washington."

For a moment, Dr. Bounpane was silent. He seemed to be struggling with himself. He sighed again. "Sooner or later Deauville was bound to learn of my conversation. I thought it best that he hear it directly from me."

"Were you afraid of what he might do when he found out?"

"Afraid?" Bounpane hesitated. "No. But this is a small state. Or perhaps I should say, the circles in which I move are tightly constricted. Do you understand?"

"Very clearly." Fallon observed the doctor keenly. "It must have been a blow when Irene Shaughnessy discharged herself."

Dr. Bounpane tapped his pipe into an ashtray. "Her case was a personal defeat. She was a bright, charming girl, with a great deal to overcome. A history of alcoholism in the family. Perhaps I let myself become too involved." He shrugged. "But then, we always tend to blame ourselves for our failures."

Dr. Bounpane rose to his feet. The interview was over.

Sarah could barely contain herself till they emerged into the mild January sunshine. "Mike McCoy!" she exclaimed as they got into the car. "I'm still reeling. And you had it worked out ahead of time. Please take two minutes to tell me what the hell is going on."

"It's simple enough in the end." Fallon sighed, as he turned on the road back to Magnolia. "Okay. The one thing we knew for sure was that an investigator had tracked down Dr. Boun-pane. Credit for that coup was assigned to Maurice Politz. But—" Fallon shrugged. "Well, you met Maurice."

The car slowed as they traveled back through the four blocks of Magnolia. "But in that case, where did Politz fit in? Obviously, he was being used as a front to hand us Bounpane's information. Which could only mean that the real source of the information had to be kept under wraps. Correct?"

Sarah nodded hesitantly. "I guess so."

"All right," Fallon continued. "So we had two mysteries. Why couldn't the real source be revealed? And the other mystery that had bothered Heidi: why was the government prosecutor so to-tally in the dark? And it occurred to me that maybe the two mysteries had the same solution."

Fallon accelerated to pass a tractor. "When I saw Oak Knoll, the pieces fell together. This is an institution for the Louisiana elite. A snooping investigator asking questions about Deauville would be reported to the Senator immediately."

"And that's what happened," Sarah interrupted. "Dr. Boun-pane called Deauville."

"That's right. And then Deauville must have called Mike McCoy and made him an offer he couldn't refuse. A brilliant move by Deauville. McCoy hands the Senator his file on Shaugh-nessy and promises to keep the information to himself. At one stroke Deauville gets the goods on Irene Shaughnessy and makes sure that the government will be sandbagged at trial."

Sarah arranged the pieces of the puzzle in her mind. "I follow you," she said. "Deauville has to find some way of presenting us with the information. He can't just tell Wolfson, 'Look what Mike McCoy gave me!' So Deauville steers us to Maurice Politz. But first he tells Politz exactly what he's looking for and when he should produce it."

"You've got it," said Fallon. "I told you it was simple." He paused to consult the map. "I was a little worried that Dr. Boun-pane might clam up when I pressed him. The man obviously be-lieves that Deauville can have him fired at will. But I was counting on a sense of loyalty to his patient."

"I still don't understand," said Sarah. "How does this all fit in with Wolfson's murder? Did Wolfson stumble on the truth?"

"We've just about got it solved," said Fallon evasively. "But for the time being you've got to be more careful than ever. Dr. Bounpane is probably already regretting his candor. By now he's probably on the phone to Deauville."

He swung the car on the ramp to the interstate.

"You don't think Deauville would do anything crazy? He'd have to kill both of us now."

"Two people are dead already," Fallon replied.

She sat back in her seat as the car ate up the miles back to New Orleans.

Part 4

Chapter 46

Fallon had just stepped into his office when Devries rolled in behind him. The patriarch was grim-faced as he slammed the door.

"Have you heard the news? No, I can see you haven't. Ken Bradley is leaving the firm."

Fallon dropped into a chair. "Why?"

"Ask him yourself. He came in yesterday and told me he had accepted an offer from White and Crystal."

White and Crystal—the elite boutique firm specializing in white-collar criminal defense. It was a logical choice for Ken, and he was a logical pick for White and Crystal. It might be happenstance that Deauville had fired White and Crystal a week before his trial.

"It's a disaster," Devries declared. "How can we go to trial in Forrest Labs?"

"Did you try to get Ken to reconsider?" Fallon asked.

"Of course. Do you think I'm a fool?"

"Did you suggest that he could lay his partnership worries to rest?"

"No. I couldn't do that."

"Why not?"

Devries faltered. "Well, I can't speak for the partnership, can I?"

179

"Can't you?" said Fallon. "If you put your weight behind him, I'd say he was a sure thing."

Devries stared straight ahead. Fallon could almost read his thoughts. After eight years at the firm, Devries barely knew Bradley. The Devries protégés had always been prep-school types like Sterling Gray. But, with Wolfson dead, Bradley was too valuable to lose. And, Devries would be thinking, Bradley would be easy to sell to the partnership. The firm's only black partner had been appointed to the court of appeals last year. Devries could play on this point.

"I'll talk to Ken," said Fallon. "I'll tell him he's guaranteed if he decides to stay."

And yet Devries seemed strangely hesitant. The logic was clear enough. Why was he balking?

"I'm not sure—" Devries began.

"Come on, St. John," Fallon insisted. "Give me your word."

Devries had turned an unattractive shade of red. "All right. Go ahead. Just get him back on the case."

He wheeled himself out of the office. Fallon scowled as he watched the wheelchair glide down the hall.

He found Bradley in his office.

"We need to talk," Fallon said.

"I'm sorry you heard about it secondhand," said Bradley. "I would have told you myself, but you were out of town."

"I want you to reconsider."

Bradley shook his head. "We can still shoot baskets together. I'll be working only a block away."

"I want you to stay."

Bradley smiled bitterly. "Are you crazy? If I wait to be canned, I'll be damaged goods."

"You won't be canned. I talked to St. John. Your partnership's in the bag."

Bradley shook his head. "I don't believe it."

"I wouldn't bullshit you."

"You don't know the whole story, Fallon."

"I know about Wolfson's evaluation."

Bradley stiffened in his chair.

"You don't need to worry about it," said Fallon. "Only Sterling and I have seen it. No one else will ever know."

Bradley stood up. His hands were trembling.

"You saw that report?"

"It was a pack of lies."

"It was worse than that. I worked my butt off for that man for eight years." Bradley's voice was unsteady. His handsome face was tight and drawn. It was hard for Fallon to recognize the easygoing powerhouse who could work all night and still have energy for a quick round of one-on-one at lunch.

"Eight years," Bradley repeated. "I came here when I was twenty-seven. Now I'm thirty-five. I spent the best years of my life pawing through documents for that man. My kids are growing up without a father. My wife sees me for an hour a day. I'm so tense I can barely sleep. And Felix Wolfson says I lack flair."

"I understand how you feel," said Fallon quietly.

Bradley's voice rose in anger. "How the hell would you know how I feel, Fallon? Are you going to tell me that the Irish didn't always have it so easy? Or is this just your general humanism speaking?"

"I don't need to be black to understand this kind of injustice."

Bradley stared at him pityingly. "You're a decent guy, Fallon. But you're way out of your depth on this one. If you knew the whole truth, you wouldn't be asking me to stay here. If you don't mind, I've got an appointment." He walked blindly down the hall.

Fallon crossed back to his own office. Bradley's voice was ringing in his ears. Fallon arced the basketball across the room. His shot was wild, six inches wide of the basket. He needed a drink. Bending down, he opened the compact refrigerator and spotted a half-empty bottle of Dr Pepper.

Before he could find a glass, Sarah came into the room.

"What's the matter with you?" Fallon asked. "You look green."

She slumped onto the couch. "I feel green. It must be that awful chicken we had for dinner on the plane last night. How are you feeling?"

"No aftereffects for me. But you might have had a bad piece."

Sarah groaned. "It must have been. But it took its time. I felt fine till about a half hour or so ago."

"Did you eat anything this morning?"

"I never eat breakfast. Just a cup of Earl Grey at home and another cup when I got to work. Peter, what are you doing?"

Fallon had pulled her to her feet. "We're going to the hospital." Grabbing her by the elbow, he marched her down the hall. "Hold that elevator," he called out.

"I don't think we should be making this much fuss," she said weakly.

Fallon had turned pale. "George Washington's only a few blocks away. I'll have you in the emergency room in a minute." He folded his arm tightly around her and pushed savagely at the elevator buttons.

Chapter 47

The man on the stretcher, a wad of cotton taped over one eye, screamed curses without interruption for ten minutes. No one appeared to notice. Finally, he lapsed into silence. The doors to the emergency room opened and closed. Through the portholes, Fallon glimpsed figures in green and white. Nothing seemed to be happening.

"You shouldn't be in here." A powerfully built nurse shouldered him aside.

"A friend of mine is inside."

"Sit in the waiting room."

Fallon folded his arms and stood his ground. The nurse began to protest, then decided he wasn't worth the effort. She hurried back into the emergency room.

Fallon harbored a deep-seated Irish mistrust for the medical profession. Hospitals were places where you went to die, or discovered that you were about to die. Inevitably, they were bound up in his mind with painful adolescent memories of his mother's final illness—long afternoons waiting in the antiquated halls of Peter Bent Brigham. Fallon sunk his hands deeper into the pockets of his jacket.

The doors flung open. A weary-looking young doctor, heavy circles under her eyes, advanced toward him.

"Mr. Fallon?"

From one look at her face, Fallon knew the worst. He put his hand against the wall to keep his knees from crumpling.

"We had to pump her stomach. I'm afraid we don't know the cause of the problem."

Fallon tried to speak, but his mouth had gone dry. "So, she's—"

"Oh, yes, Ms. Strasser is doing fine. We'll just keep her over-night to be sure there are no complications. If you'll stop at the desk outside, there's some paperwork we need you to fill out."

At the mention of paperwork, the man on the stretcher launched into a new stream of obscenity.

With a reassuring nod to Fallon, the doctor disappeared back through the double doors.

Weak with relief, Fallon walked back to the waiting room. As he finished signing the last of several forms, Sterling Gray stepped through the entrance. Looking around worriedly, he spotted Fallon at the desk.

"Is she all right? They said it was some kind of food poisoning."

"She'll be fine," said Fallon. "They're just keeping her over-night as a precaution."

"Can I see her?"

"I don't think she's ready to see anyone. There's nothing for us to do here right now."

Together, they walked out onto Pennsylvania Avenue. After hours of hospital air, the sharp wind was a relief.

"You don't have a coat," Gray said. "I'll call a cab."

Fallon shook his head. "I need the walk."

"I came down as soon as I heard," said Gray as they crossed Washington Circle to New Hampshire Avenue. For a moment he was silent. "Sarah and I are actually more than friends. Or we were. She broke it off."

Fallon said nothing.

"When I thought something might have happened to her, I just had to be there." Gray stared down uncomfortably. "I should have told you about Sarah and me. But we kept it a secret from everyone."

"It's hard to keep that sort of thing a secret," said Fallon quietly.

Gray glanced at him quickly. "You knew?"

"Pretty much, yes."

"I guess that makes me an even bigger ass. If you're going to conduct a secret romance, at least keep it secret."

"There's no such thing as a secret. Not in a firm like ours."

Gray put a hand on his arm. "Watch it there. You almost walked into a car."

"Don't worry about me. The important thing is that Sarah's okay."

"She could be dead, if it weren't for you," said Gray. "She owes you a lot."

They had reached the entrance of their building. As they stepped into the warmth, Fallon realized that he was chilled through.

"You should take the rest of the day off," said Gray as they arrived at the eighth floor. "We can get together on Forrest Labs tomorrow."

"I've got a few loose ends to tie up," said Fallon. "Forrest Labs is going to have wait a little."

Back in his office, he found the half-empty bottle of Dr Pepper on his desk where he had left it. Fallon opened the bottle, then held it up to his nose. There was no odor. Fallon closed the top tightly and put the bottle in an empty drawer.

At least he had saved Sarah, even if he had been too late for Heidi. With her usual otherworldly clarity of mind, Heidi Hollings had seen the simple solution to the mystery. He heard again the sound of Heidi's lilting, irreverent laugh. Why hadn't the fool understood the dangers of confronting a murderer? It was time to tie up the loose ends.

Fallon called Accounting.

"I need some phone records right away. The bills for Devries, Wolfson, Gray, and Bradley."

"What month do you need?"

"The second half of last year. Six months worth."

Fallon could sense the perplexity at the other end. "I'm sorry,

Mr. Fallon. We don't keep all those records here. I'll have to get them back from storage. I can have them first thing tomorrow."

Fallon hesitated. "There won't be any glitches?"

"They'll be on your desk by ten."

Fallon sat back, frustrated. He sent the basketball swishing through the net. He reached for the phone again, then decided that a surprise visit might produce better results. Bundling up in the tweed coat, he walked over to the plush offices of White and Crystal at Farragut Square.

Chapter 48

Bertram White came out to the reception area to greet him.

"Mr. F! Looking your usual shaggy self. Come on in."

"I like your new digs," Fallon observed as they passed a glass-walled conference room hung with Oriental tapestries. White's own office was twice the size of Fallon's ample quarters.

"Jesus, Bertie," he said, "You could set up a basketball court in here."

White laughed. "What can I do for you? I warn you, there's no point in twisting my arm. I've been trying to get Ken Bradley for years. You guys have the missed the boat. He's going to be one of the greats."

"You're dead right," said Fallon. "But I had something a little different in mind. When I heard Ken had accepted your offer, I started thinking again about the Deauville trial."

The breezy expression vanished from White's face. "How's that exactly?"

"I'm sure you haven't entirely forgotten the case," said Fallon dryly. "I want to know why Deauville fired you a week before the trial."

"Let's not think of it as firing. Let's call it a parting of the ways."

"Okay," said Fallon. "An amicable divorce. Now tell me why."

"I seem to remember reading about something called

attorney-client privilege," said White. "If Deauville won't tell you, I don't see how I can."

"All right," said Fallon, "let's take it step by step. "Your firm has its own full-time investigators. I know them. They're very good people. But I read their reports when I took over the case. They didn't turn up much."

"They found the stuff on Deauville's new bimbo. What was her name? Lucy Wellington, wasn't it? The one he took up with after Andrea Callas. You made a little bit of hay with that at the trial, playing the jealousy angle. Andrea Callas takes the revenge of the spurned lover."

Fallon nodded. "Your investigators were pretty good on the Andrea Callas end of the case. Not so good on Irene Shaughnessy."

"No," White acknowledged. "But it wasn't their priority."

"Be that as it may," said Fallon, "let me put this to you as a hypothetical. Some time in August or September, Deauville came to you and told you he had hired his own P.I. He claimed to have some hot stuff on Irene Shaughnessy."

White shrugged his shoulders. "I'm listening."

"I can't be sure exactly how this conversation went," said Fallon, "but, after all, this is only a hypothetical. I'm imagining that you did just what I would have done. I would have turned the material over to my own people to verify and cross-check. If there were any letters or affidavits, I'd want to meet the author of those documents myself."

White nodded to show he was following the story line.

"But then Deauville did something unaccountable. He refused to let you have access to his P.I. You could have the end product, but that was it. At first it seemed like a minor problem. But Deauville wouldn't yield an inch. Then, who knows. Maybe you were fed up with him anyway. Maybe you smelled a rat. Or maybe he was tired of your scruples. Anyway, the thing blew up. The next thing you know, Deauville is sitting in Felix Wolfson's office."

White stood up and slowly paced the room. "You say you've never talked to Deauville about this?"

"Never."

White gazed thoughtfully at the Japanese triptych screen that

dominated the wall across from his desk. "Well," he concluded,
"I'm glad you decided to present me with a purely hypothetical
scenario. I don't need to tell you, of all people, how seriously I
regard the sanctity of the attorney-client relationship. I think you
understand my situation entirely."

Fallon stood also. "Absolutely. Thanks, Bertie. I'll see myself
out."

On Connecticut, Fallon hailed a cab for Georgetown. Mrs.
Muller, Wolfson's German housekeeper, admitted him into the
house.

"Has anyone been to visit?" Fallon asked.

"If they had, I would have informed you as instructed," she
replied stiffly.

"I just wanted to be sure."

"There have been no visitors."

Fallon went up the stairs to Wolfson's library.

He had no idea what he was looking for. But this was his last
chance before he turned the case over to the police. He had no
illusions about the resources they would devote to the investigation. He needed to hand them as tight a case as possible.

By seven o'clock, he was satisfied that he had scanned every
piece of paper in the room. The excursion had uncovered yet
more unsavory sidelights into Wolfson's activities. But nothing
germane.

It was time to get over to the hospital before visiting hours
ended. As he put on his coat, Fallon focused again on the peculiar PC on the side table, which appeared to operate without a
keyboard. Where the keyboard should have been, there was just
a single control stick. Fallon reached to the side of the console
and found the power switch. The screen brightened. A menu
appeared. Fallon was offered his choice of "Calendar," "Check-
book," and "Wordperfect." He tried the joystick but nothing
happened.

He was stumped. Wolfson was no computer buff. At work he
dictated to Fran Rendelman. Fallon was surprised that Wolfson
even bothered with a PC at home.

Then he remembered. It had been late last summer, just before the Deauville trial blew up. Wolfson had won a major anti-

trust case for a new client—a budding Silicon Valley manufacturer. In addition to his munificent fee, Wolfson had received, as a token of gratitude, a prototype for a voice-operated PC.

So this must be it. But what the hell did voice-operated really mean? Fallon scrutinized the menu on the screen. Feeling a little bit foolish, he said aloud, "Wordperfect."

Nothing happened.

Maybe you had to press the joystick while you spoke. Fallon tried again. Once more, no result. Did you have to say please? Or recite a password? Fallon felt like a student in a language lab. "The rain in Spain falls mainly in the plain."

He paused. Could the computer be having trouble with his Boston accent? With the model of Henry Higgins before him, Fallon articulated loudly and clearly, "Wordperfect."

The screen dissolved. A new message appeared. "You have no Wordperfect files. Do you wish to create a file?"

"No," Fallon replied.

The screen returned to the original menu.

Had Wolfson ever used his new toy? Or was it just another trophy? "Calendar," he said loudly.

A new message flashed on the screen. "What date please?"

"December 21." The date of Wolfson's murder.

A calendar page appeared. With no entries. Apparently Wolfson hadn't troubled to use this feature, either.

Then Fallon realized that, of course, he was looking at December 21 of *this* year. He reentered his command, this time specifying the correct year.

After a few seconds, a new screen appeared showing one entry for the day of Wolfson's death—the gala charity performance of the *Nutcracker* at the Kennedy Center. Evidently Wolfson didn't bother to note office appointments on his home calendar.

Fallon politely requested December 20.

Dinner with Jeff Unruh of Forrest Labs at Maison Blanche.

December 19. Breakfast at Duke Ziebert's with Cicero Deauville. Dinner party at Margot Kellerman's.

Fallon paged back slowly to the beginning of September when Wolfson had started using his electronic diary. From the end of the trial in September, until December 19, there was no mention of Deauville. Or Maurice Politz, Dr. Bounpane, or Mike McCoy.

But there was breakfast at Duke Ziebert's. The timing was just right.

"Goodbye," he said, "and thanks for the help." The computer made no response.

Chapter 49

Sarah stared into the darkness of her hospital room. Her throat ached and her stomach felt like hell. But the physical discomfort was nothing beside the pulsing fear that kept her awake despite all the Demerol.

Someone had tried to kill her. And they would try again. It might be anything she ate or drank. Or, like Heidi, she might be shot in the chest. Or stabbed. Or strangled.

She had to get hold of herself. After all, Fallon seemed confident enough. He had sat with her for an hour that evening, reporting the latest developments. In another day, he insisted, he would have it all wrapped up. In the meantime, she would go home, watch the soaps, and catch up on her sleep.

Sarah shuddered. They had taken her watch. How many more hours before they came to let her out? Exhausted, she fell back onto the pillows and into a troubled sleep.

It seemed like only minutes later when she was awakened for breakfast. Much, much later a friendly resident popped in with her chart.

"How are you feeling?" he asked.

"Awful."

He laughed. "Good. You're right on schedule. It'll be a couple of days before you start getting back to normal. I want you to stay in bed and stick to liquids. Open your mouth." He popped in a thermometer.

At nine, Fallon arrived to take her home. The nurse insisted on wheeling her to the hospital entrance.

"I can walk," she protested.

"It's the rules, dear."

The wheelchair bumped across the threshold of the elevator. The nurse maneuvered her into a corner. So this is what Devries goes through every day, she reflected. What a fate for a sportsman.

Downstairs, Fallon helped her out of the wheelchair and walked her to the door. She stopped in amazement. Overnight, the city had been transformed. Pennsylvania Avenue was blanketed in snow, and thick spirals were swirling down from a leaden sky.

"Hold on tight," said Fallon as he slammed the door of their cab. "No one in Washington can deal with snow. Half the city's already shut down. And the other half will close soon." He turned to the cabdriver. "Think you can manage? It's just a few blocks."

The driver glanced in the mirror. "You're not the only one who knows how to drive in the snow, buddy."

Fallon burst into laughter. The driver's Boston accent was a match for his own. As other cars skidded and stalled, the taxi glided down Pennsylvania like a horse-drawn sleigh.

"They're calling this a blizzard," said the driver disparagingly. "In Boston, this would be a flurry."

"That's the attitude," said Fallon. They drew up in front of Sarah's building. "Just wait a second and I'll be right back."

The lobby door was propped open by a snow shovel. The doorman was not in evidence. Lucy, the desk clerk, greeted Sarah with a pile of mail. "Henry disappeared twenty minutes ago," she said. "I guess his shovel's the last we're going to see of him today." She shook her head. "I'll be taking off myself. School's canceled and I got three kids at home."

On the tenth floor, Sarah was grateful that Fallon had insisted on accompanying her upstairs. What if someone were waiting on the other side of the door?

She turned the key in the lock. The empty apartment yawned at her.

"You going to be all right?" Fallon asked. "I can get someone to keep you company."

Sarah shook her head. "I'll be okay." It still hurt to talk.

"I'll take your word for it. But call if you change your mind. I'll be back at dinner bearing milkshakes." With a wave, he strode down the hall to the elevator.

Sarah was startled by a purring at her feet. In the traumas of the last day, she had forgotten about Popcorn. She hurried guiltily to the kitchen. But fresh food and water had already been set out. Fallon had remembered.

Still muffled in her down coat, Sarah slid open the glass doors and stepped onto the balcony.

The storm showed no sign of letting up. From the look of the thick gray clouds, it might snow for hours. Far below, the deck was barely visible through the driving swirls.

Retreating to the warmth, she lowered herself slowly into an armchair. Popcorn jumped into her lap and lazily closed his eyes. As Sarah gently scratched the cat between the ears, she felt his body vibrate in a low purr.

Daylight had chased away the terrors of the night. In the cold light of morning, there were no mysteries. The chain of events was clear. Mike McCoy had uncovered the dirt on Irene Shaughnessy. Deauville had bribed McCoy to withhold the dynamite from the prosecutor.

But Deauville still needed to deal with his own attorneys. Bertram White, scenting trouble, had refused to play ball. Felix Wolfson was another story. Wolfson would accept Maurice Politz without question.

Had Wolfson guessed the whole truth from the beginning? Or did he stumble on to it later? Either way, Wolfson, the insatiable tormentor, had decided to put the screws to Deauville. But for once he had met his match. The snake had struck back.

Huddled in the chair, Sarah could feel Deauville's hot breath against her cheek, his mouth at her breast.

Sarah put a hand to her forehead. It was burning hot. At the hospital her temperature had been normal. She drew the down coat more tightly around her.

Heidi had confronted Deauville with her deductions. Maybe she had even seen Deauville in Wolfson's office on the day of the murder. For once, Heidi's audacity had proved fatal. Deauville had responded with his usual ruthless efficiency. And he would have gotten away with it, if Sarah had not known Heidi's habits so well.

No doubt Deauville thought he was out of the woods. Till Maurice Politz or Dr. Bounpane called in with news of Fallon's inquiries. Within twenty-four hours, Deauville had struck again with poison in her tea.

Sarah lifted Popcorn to the floor. She wasn't scared now. She was angry. The Honorable Senator Cicero Deauville had tried to rape her. Then he had tried to kill her. But he had failed. And this time, no legal miracle would save his skin.

She was tired of being a victim. With her heart pounding, she reached for the phone. It took a while, but she was finally put through. She smiled as she heard the surprise in his voice. But of course he would see her.

You bet you'll see me, said Sarah fiercely to herself as she hung up the phone.

She called to the lobby desk for a cab, but there was no answer. Then she remembered that Lucy was leaving to take care of her kids.

Fine, she'd get a cab at the hotel on the next block. Her head was throbbing. In the bathroom, she splashed some cold water on her face. Her cheeks were flushed and her eyes rimmed red.

For a moment she almost lost her resolve. It was madness to rush out into the storm. What did she think she could accomplish?

Then the need to confront Deauville, to hear him lie and beg, became too compelling. With a final goodbye to Popcorn, she headed for the street.

Chapter 50

The trip to the capitol, normally a ten-minute drive, took nearly an hour. Government offices had closed. The entire civil service was in exodus. As Fallon had observed, Washington drivers were helpless in the snow. At every other corner, an accident snarled traffic.

Sarah had been shivering in her apartment. Now she was soaked in perspiration. She tried to let some fresh air into the stifling cab, which smelled of day-old curry. But her window wouldn't budge, and the turbaned driver only shook his head when she sought his help.

Despite the storm, the Dirksen office building was humming with activity. Staffers popped in and out of Deauville's offices. Sarah presented herself to the receptionist, an ash-blonde in her mid-twenties. Another conquest for Deauville, Sarah thought.

"Sarah Strasser. The Senator is expecting me."

"Oh, Miss Strasser." Another Louisiana accent. "The Senator has some people in with him. Why don't you take a seat?"

Half an hour passed. An unopened magazine fell from her lap to the floor. Sarah straightened herself in her chair.

"Are you all right?" asked the receptionist.

Before Sarah could reply, five buzzers sounded in quick succession. "Now he'll go shooting out of here," the receptionist sighed. "Seven and a half minutes to roll call."

She had hardly finished when Deauville emerged into the reception area, straightening his tie. He made straight for the door, taking no notice of Sarah.

"That's bad luck," said the receptionist. "Now he won't be back for at least an hour."

Sarah didn't have an hour's strength left in her. She followed Deauville into the hall. The Senator had disappeared around a corner. At the sound of her voice, he stopped dead.

He faced her unsmilingly. "I have to get to the floor. I'll be back."

"I have to talk to you now."

Deauville glanced around the corridor as if trying to decide whether Sarah would cause a scene. He decided to rely on charm. The cold expression left his face. The clear blue eyes crinkled at the corners.

"You just come with me," he said. "We'll take the underground shuttle over to the Capitol. After the vote we'll have a nice long chat."

Ignoring his offered arm, Sarah followed him into the elevator. In the basement, the elevator opened onto a small platform. Rail tracks disappeared into a tunnel. A mini-tram car filled with senators was gliding away. It was the nation's most privileged transportation system.

Another car rolled up immediately. As soon as they were seated, they started off alone on the short journey underneath Capitol Hill.

Deauville patted her hand. "I'm glad you called. I felt terrible when you left so suddenly that night." He smiled. "It's so easy to have misunderstandings at the start of a relationship."

Sarah's mind reeled at this bland, untroubled denial of all that had happened. The speech she had carefully rehearsed in the taxi flew out of her mind.

"You tried to rape me," she said. The simple statement of truth was all she could manage.

"Shh," said Deauville pleasantly. "That's no way for my lawyer to talk. Someone might overhear and not realize you were joking."

"You're not going to get away with it," she said.

Deauville's eyes turned steely in the dim light. "I'd be very careful with your accusations. A young lawyer who dates her clients and then accuses them of assault could easily do irreparable damage to her career." He picked up her hand again and squeezed it sharply.

Sarah flinched. "I have the evidence this time. I know all about Mike McCoy and Maurice Politz. And I know that you killed Wolfson when he tried to blackmail you."

Deauville laughed. "My dear Sarah, you're insane."

The handsome face before her was swimming. Sarah struggled to focus. "You're the one who's insane. How many women did you think you could rape before you were convicted?"

"You're my lawyer," said Deauville. "You ought to know."

"Did you really think you could bribe McCoy and get away with it?" She shook her head. "Too many people were involved— McCoy, Politz, Dr. Bounpane."

Deauville smiled. "I don't think any of those gentlemen will have a word to say against me. Ridiculous to think that a man like Mike McCoy could be bribed."

Sarah felt herself giving way before Deauville's unshakable confidence. "Felix Wolfso—" she began.

"Wolfson?" Deauville cut in. "Do you honestly think Felix Wolfson would try to cross me? I opened doors for that man, and he would have kissed my boots to keep it that way."

Deauville shook his head. "Go back to law review, Miss Strasser. Better still, become a psychologist. Don't try to play with the big boys. You'll just get hurt."

They had reached the end of the line.

"You tried to kill me," said Sarah.

"Listen," said Deauville. "Did I say become a psychologist? I should have said, see a psychologist. You need help." He jumped out of the carriage and headed for the senate floor.

Sarah wandered aimlessly through basement corridors. Deauville had reduced her to a stammering child. She had been a fool to confront him today. She should be in bed.

Spying a group of staffers, she followed them up a series of stairs to the rotunda. The traffic had disappeared from the streets outside. In the falling snow, the city was silent. Teenagers on cross-country skis schussed down the center of East Capitol Street. Sarah trudged down Independence Avenue to the Metro.

Slipping on an icy patch, she hurtled onto her face. For a moment she thought she might not have the strength to get up. Then she thought, in a few hours this will all be over. Peter will come by with milkshakes. We'll watch the storm from the balcony.

With a sudden effort, she heaved herself to her feet, brushed off the worst of the snow, and resumed her trek.

Chapter 51

When she finally reached home, she dropped her sodden clothes on the floor, heaped every blanket she owned on the bed, and crawled underneath. The shaking refused to stop. Popcorn perched on the edge of the mattress purring, enjoying the new game.

The phone on the night table rang. She picked it up to speak to Fallon.

"Listen," said Deauville. "I want to apologize. You've been under a lot of strain. I didn't behave like a gentleman just now."

"Don't talk to me about gentlemen."

"I'm coming over."

"The hell you are."

Deauville chuckled. "Put your mind at rest. I've lost interest in a romantic liaison. But I can't have you going around town accusing me of murder. We have to get some things straight."

"Stay away from me."

"I won't be long."

The line went dead.

Sarah tried to sit up. The room shifted unsteadily. She dialed Fallon.

His voice mail clicked on. Of course. The secretaries would have gone home. She left a short message and hung up.

It would take Deauville an hour to get across town. Maybe

200

more. Would he force his way in? Sarah had no illusions about the lock on her door. Once, when she had locked herself out, Ken Bradley had popped the lock with a credit card.

She picked up the phone and called Bradley. Again, she left a message.

Sarah looked at her watch. Ten minutes since Deauville had hung up. Taking a deep breath, she called Sterling Gray.

"Hello." It was a female voice.

"I'm sorry," said Sarah, "I think I've dialed the wrong number."

There was a ripple of laughter at the other end. "Don't be certain. Who are you trying to reach?"

"Sterling Gray."

"Then you've succeeded after all." The voice turned away from the receiver. "Sterling, a charming young lady on the phone for you. I've got to look after St. John." Only then did it occur to Sarah that her interlocutor was Charlotte Devries.

"Sterling," she said. "I'm sorry to call you like this. But I need you to come over right now."

Gray's familiar voice was reassuring. "I'll be right there. It was irresponsible for the hospital to let you out."

"It's not that," said Sarah. "I'll explain when you get here. Don't think I'm crazy, Sterling, but Cicero Deauville is coming over here and I think he's going to kill me."

There was silence at the other end.

"I know how it sounds," Sarah pleaded, "but just come on over. Please?"

"Just sit tight," said Gray. "I'm leaving right now."

Sarah sank back on the pillows in relief. Too often she had been unfair to Sterling Gray. He was an easy man to take for granted. But he came through when the chips were down. Though he probably thought Sarah's fever had left her delusional.

Moving very carefully, Sarah stepped out of bed and pulled on a dressing gown. How would Sterling react when she told him the whole story? Incredulity?

Tugging a comforter behind her, Sarah made her way to the living room and dropped into an armchair. It seemed an eternity since New Year's Eve when Sterling had asked her to marry him in this room.

Poor Sterling, she thought. His ex-wife dined at the White House with her diamonds and her power-broker husband while Sterling's life was shot to hell. His rebuff by a first-year associate must have been the last straw.

Still, now that she was in trouble, Sterling knew how to set aside his grievances. She had underestimated him.

Footsteps sounded in the hall. She heard Sterling's knock on the door.

"Come in," she said. "It's open."

Chapter 52

Fallon felt his temper flaring. "You promised me those phone records today."

"*I* didn't promise anything. You didn't talk to *me*."

Fallon bit his lip. "Could you send a messenger over to storage to get the bills right away?"

"No messengers today because of the snow."

In the end, Fallon arranged to pick up the records himself. Diamond Cab obligingly located his Boston cabbie. Together, they skidded skillfully to the warehouse on New York Avenue near the Arboretum.

To Fallon's renewed annoyance, no one had bothered to locate the files. Another half hour was wasted. His stomach growled. He had skipped breakfast and lunch and it was nearly two.

Finally, an employee lackadaisically deposited a crate at his feet and disappeared into the recesses of the cavernous warehouse.

Fallon ripped open the carton and tore through the stacks of printouts. The bills had been filed without regard to any obvious principle of organization. After much searching, he established stacks on the stained concrete floor. St. John Devries, Felix Wolfson, Sterling Gray, and Ken Bradley. When the papers were sorted, Fallon began searching through each stack in turn, beginning with Wolfson.

The "504" New Orleans area code flashed out at him immediately. Wolfson had called Maurice Politz repeatedly in mid-December. Judging from the brevity of the calls, Politz had successfully avoided him.

So, Fallon reflected, Wolfson had been hot on the conspirators' trail. Politz might have eluded him temporarily. But by December 19, Wolfson was sure enough of his ground to confront Deauville over breakfast at Duke Ziebert's. Two days later he was dead.

Wolfson's records yielded no more clues. Not a single New Orleans call before December.

Fallon continued his search. It was freezing on the warehouse floor. But he had to be sure he was right.

There it was. In the dim light he squinted at the columns on the AT&T printout. Finally. He looked from one sheet to another, checking yet one more time.

The first call to Maurice Politz. Not from Wolfson, of course. Wolfson had never spoken to the bumbling investigator before December.

No, the first call from the firm to Maurice Politz had come on September 12, the day before Cicero Deauville had appeared in Wolfson's office. On September 12, when Wolfson had no inkling of the prize case that was about to drop into his lap.

Fallon sank back onto the cold concrete. It was as he thought. Bertie White had spotted Deauville's scam. He had confronted his client. A week before his trial, Deauville had left White and Crystal in search of more malleable attorneys.

But the Senator had to be sure that his new firm would play ball. Before he arrived at Arant and Devries, Deauville made certain that there would be no questions about Maurice Politz and his evidence. No one from Arant and Devries would actually meet Dr. Bounpane. There would be no danger that Wolfson or Fallon might learn that Mike McCoy, and not Maurice Politz, had discovered the skeleton in Irene Shaughnessy's closet. The evidence at trial would be a bombshell. The prosecutor would be caught flatfooted.

The taxi slalommed back down New York Avenue. Somehow

Wolfson had put the pieces together. For once he overplayed his hand. It had cost him his life.

The streets were almost empty now, but the heavy cab glided along effortlessly. The clues had been there all along. If he had understood their significance, Heidi might still be alive.

Fallon's mind traveled back to the drama of the Deauville trial, to the day he had cross-examined Andrea Callas. He saw again the anxious faces of the defense team assembled for a tense lunch in the conference room. The talk had turned to Irene Shaughnessy. Would the judge allow her testimony? Suddenly, a causal remark brought the discussion to a dead stop. What were the exact words? That Fallon could easily discredit Irene Shaughnessy as "a spoiled brat or an Irish alcoholic." That "it would be child's play to tear her apart on the stand."

What a faux pas that had been, laughing about Irish alcoholics in front of Peter Fallon. Everyone had blushed for Fallon's sake.

But no one at that anxious luncheon yet knew that Irene Shaughnessy was an alcoholic. None of the lawyers had heard of the Oak Knoll Sanatorium or Dr. Bounpane. Wolfson wouldn't receive Politz's dynamite report for several more hours.

The remark was more than a faux pas. It should have been a fatal slip, if anyone had understood its significance. The episode had lingered in his memory, waiting to be understood.

The crash jolted Fallon from his reproaches. By the time he straightened up, the cabbie was already out of the car and on the street.

"What in Christ's name do you think you're doing, lady? This is a one-way street!"

Fallon stepped out into the swirling snow. A Volvo station wagon, skidding around the corner, had sideswiped the cab, sending it on to the sidewalk.

In the heavy snow it was impossible to tell where he was. He looked around for a street sign. K and 15th. With luck he could walk to Sarah's building in less than an hour. He would break the news to her first. Then it would be time for the police.

Pressing a small fortune into the cabbie's hand, Fallon turned up the collar of his tweed coat and plunged into the storm.

Chapter 53

The door swung open. Sterling Gray stepped into the room. A lingering fringe of snow formed epaulets on the shoulders of his coat. He studied Sarah with concern.

"How could the hospital discharge you? You look like you're burning up."

He crossed the room to the armchair where she huddled under a comforter and placed a cold hand on her forehead. "Is there a thermometer in the medicine cabinet?"

Sarah nodded. Gray fetched the thermometer and pored carefully over the directions. "I never trust these digital things," he said. "I miss the old-fashioned models."

"Sterling," Sarah said. "I know you think I'm crazy. But what I said about Deauville is true. He's dangerous."

"Be quiet and put this in your mouth." He placed the thermometer under her tongue. "You can tell me about Deauville some other time. For the moment, your biggest worry is your fever."

He examined the gauge. "102.4."

"Try it again," said Sarah. "It couldn't be that high."

But the second reading was identical.

"That does it," said Gray. "As soon as the storm lets up, we're taking you back to the hospital."

"They don't admit you just because you're running a temperature."

"I don't think you grasp how ill you are." Gray placed a reassuring hand on her shoulder. "But we'll take care of that. When was the last time you ate?"

Sarah tried to remember. "Breakfast at the hospital."

Gray was horrified. "Are you trying to do yourself in? I'll get you something."

"I'm not hungry. Really."

"Your wishes don't come into this. I'll make you something light. And you're going to eat it."

Sterling disappeared into the kitchen. Sarah sank back gratefully and watched the snow swirl on the terrace.

Her thoughts drifted aimlessly. Maybe the thermometer was correct after all. She remembered her first glimpse of Sterling Gray when she interviewed at the firm. A gentle man, she thought at the time, with a nice sense of humor. Her mind flashed to his bejeweled ex-wife at the White House dinner table, to his son, demanding Heidi's food at the Red Sage. Sterling deserved better.

Sarah wondered if things between them might have worked out differently if Cicero Deauville hadn't appeared on the scene. Sterling had always been in competition with the Senator. He had made his first overtures during the trial, just as Deauville was capturing her foolish imagination. In a sense, she had never taken Sterling seriously.

Heidi had never held him in much regard. Sarah would never forget her crack about Sterling's weak chin and her comment that he was "no smarter than he needed to be." But that was like Heidi.

How long ago it seemed since Heidi first walked into her office the evening of the Andrea Callas cross-examination. Sterling had dropped in as well, still in his running clothes. He suggested that she be a "big sister" to Heidi.

But what an irritating girl Heidi had been that first evening. Heidi had followed her out when she left to meet Deauville at the Palm. Across the street, Sterling Gray was talking to an athletic young man. Heidi had made some irritating crack about that, too. The feel of that September evening, of Dupont Circle in the dusk, flooded back with Proustian immediacy. The blurry video of her recollections crystallized suddenly into sharp focus.

She saw again the image of Sterling Gray and his companion. For a single piercing moment the picture froze full-frame in her memory.

She felt as if she were falling. Falling into a bottomless pit of terror. But she kept her wits enough to stifle the scream that was bursting from inside her.

Because the athletic young man in Dupont Circle was no longer a stranger. He was Mike McCoy, the government investigator. And that September evening, he had no business talking to anybody on the Deauville defense team.

Sarah's heart was beating wildly. She looked around the living room as if searching for an escape. In the kitchen, the kettle had come to a boil.

There had been no flash of recognition when Sarah met McCoy in the U.S. Attorney's office. But Heidi, of course, must have made the connection at once. And that one clue had been enough. Heidi had been fool enough to confront Sterling. Two days later, she was dead.

Tears welled up in her eyes.

"I've made you some tea and toast. That won't be too much for your system."

Sterling set the tray by her side.

"Are you crying? Listen, don't worry. You're going to be fine."

Sarah nodded. *Behave naturally,* she thought.

"Have some tea," he urged. "Come on now." He placed the cup of Earl Grey in her hands.

She looked down at the steaming cup, drank in its fragrance. Her eyes rose to meet Sterling's. There could be no doubt. Sterling had tried once before. This time he meant to succeed.

"I'm feeling sick. I can't drink anything."

"You can get some down," he insisted. It was the voice he had used in trying to persuade his intractable child.

"I'll be sick."

"It's good for you."

Gray put his hand on hers and raised the cup to her lips.

"Here we go."

With her last strength, Sarah pushed the cup away. The hot liquid splashed onto the comforter.

Their eyes met again. Sterling understood at once.

"There was no point in making a mess," he said calmly. "There's plenty more in the pot. And you'll drink some before I leave."

She tried to shake her head. "It's over, Sterling."

"For you. Not for me."

"Fallon knows," she said weakly. "Nothing can save you."

Gray's face knotted in worry. Then, surprisingly, he smiled. "You know, I'd almost forgotten about Fallon." He dropped in the facing chair. "Fallon isn't invulnerable. I'm dealing with him."

"He knows."

Gray smiled. "I'll just have to take my chances."

This is the last face I'll see, thought Sarah suddenly. The thought was unbearable. Perhaps, if they kept talking, Deauville would arrive. But what help would he provide?

"Deauville paid you?" Speaking was becoming difficult. Her throat felt as though she had swallowed a handful of hot coals. The room was swimming before her eyes.

The question seemed to irritate Sterling. "Of course he paid me. Why else would I do it? Everyone knew I was in hock to those damn divorce lawyers."

Sarah said nothing. This appeared to infuriate him.

"You have no right to pass judgment on me. You think I did anything different from Felix Wolfson? He knew in his gut that Deauville was guilty. We were paid to obstruct justice. And we each did our part."

Sarah hoped he would continue. But he lapsed into silence. Sarah could see his eyes move toward the steaming teapot. What deadly poison had he used this time?

"Wolfson found out?" Her voice came out as a croak.

Gray nodded. "I don't know how. He talked to Deauville first. Met him for breakfast. Deauville didn't care. He knew Wolfson wouldn't expose him. The scandal would take Wolfson down, too. Besides, Deauville could do a lot for Wolfson."

Sterling smiled bitterly. "I don't think Wolfson gave a damn about the morals of the whole thing. He probably liked the idea of buying the government investigator. But he couldn't stand the idea that Deauville had gone behind his back. If Wolfson couldn't punish Deauville, he'd wreak his vengeance on me. He'd make sure I never worked in this town again."

Sterling pleaded for understanding. "What should I have done? Let him ruin me?"

"Heidi?" Sarah forced the word out. Soon she would collapse entirely. Sterling would force some tea down her throat. It would all be over.

"The little fool," said Sterling. "Why the hell couldn't she mind her own business? She gave me forty-eight hours before she went to the police. I was frantic. I bought a gun in a pawn shop. Naturally, no questions asked.

"I didn't have a plan. But then I saw her jogging as I drove to pick up dinner that night. She got right into the car when I stopped. It was almost too easy."

Sarah tried to speak.

"I can't hear you," said Sterling.

"I thought you were a decent guy."

Sterling seemed to search for an answer. His face filled suddenly with pain.

"I thought so, too," he said. "Decent. Law-abiding. I even paid my parking tickets. But I've learned. We'll do what's needed to survive."

He pulled his chair up to her own. Sarah shrank back, but his face loomed before her. "I *was* a decent guy. I did everything I was supposed to.

"Don't you understand? It was them—my wife, Wolfson, even Heidi. I didn't ask for any of this. You can see that? Can't you?"

What does he want? Sarah wondered. Absolution? Understanding? It was too great an effort to keep her eyes open. When they closed, Sterling would finish with her.

But when Sarah looked up again, Sterling was staring past her. Someone else had entered the room. There was conversation, but Sarah couldn't make out the words. She tried desperately to turn her head, but the effort was too great.

A gun appeared to grow out of Sterling's hand. So, after all, she would go the same way as Heidi. There was some small comfort in that.

Sterling was backing slowly toward the balcony. The bullet would be painless. It would be over in a moment. A single tear rolled down her cheek.

A sharp gust ripped through the room as the sliding-glass door opened. What was happening? Sterling had reached the edge of the narrow balcony. In slow motion, he swung one leg over the balustrade. Then the other. His eyes looked into hers. Then he was gone.

The last thing she saw before her eyes closed was the anxious face of Peter Fallon.

"I'm all right," Sarah said. But no words came out.

Fallon felt for a pulse. It was jumpy but strong. He put her hand underneath the comforter. Reluctantly, he stepped out on to the balcony.

The gun lay on the balustrade. Sterling had gone to his death unarmed. Fallon pocketed the weapon. The police would need it to close out Heidi's case.

Despite the cold, sweat poured off his forehead, blurring his vision. Sterling had moved so deliberately, with no sign of desperation, like a man setting out on a walk. The moment that Fallon entered the room, Sterling had accepted his end. Perhaps he even embraced it.

The storm was spent. The winds were dying. But snowflakes still fell faintly on the hushed streets of the capitol and on the body of Sterling Gray at rest in the snow.

Epilogue

Although the forsythia were already blooming along the Georgetown canal, the brisk March wind was distinctly unspringlike. On this bright morning, Sarah had the towpath almost to herself.

Some of the old woodframe town houses that lined the edge of the path had been converted to shops. Occasional brass plates announced small businesses or consulting operations. Checking the numbers carefully, she spotted the discreet shingle.

PETER FALLON
ATTORNEY AT LAW

Sarah climbed the uncarpeted stairs. The door at the top was open. The reception area was empty, though there was evidence of work in progress. A large room to her right was bare. From the office to her left came the sound of Fallon talking on the phone. She let her eyes wander around the high-ceilinged rooms. No sign of upscale renovation here. Or even a paint job.

Fallon came hurrying out of his office, dressed in his fisherman's sweater and jeans. His face lighted up when he saw her.

"How do you like it?"

"Well," Sarah hesitated. "It's different."

Fallon laughed. "Come see my headquarters."

She followed him into his office, half filled with unpacked boxes. A old oak desk faced grimy widows with a lovely view of the canal. The basketball hoop had been installed over a window seat.

"Eventually I'm going to get the place painted," Fallon assured her. "But one thing at a time." He looked out the streaky windows. "It's a beautiful morning. Let's take a walk before lunch."

They turned up the towpath in the direction of Great Falls. The sun struggled out from behind a cloud. Sarah fished in her bag for sunglasses.

She hadn't seen Fallon since his departure from the firm, shortly after she was released from the hospital. Rumors circulated as to his whereabouts. Fallon had joined Ken Bradley at White and Crystal; he had returned to the Justice Department; he had moved to the West Coast. Then, out of the blue, he called to propose lunch.

"I saw the new Deauville indictment," said Sarah. "I hope they don't let Ingrid Torval prosecute this time."

"I don't know," said Fallon. "She almost deserves the chance. Anyway, this is one trial Deauville isn't walking away from."

"Did you hear that Forrest Labs has followed Ken Bradley to White and Crystal?"

Fallon laughed. "I played basketball with Ken and Bertie White last week. Ken is a god over there now. Rainmaker-in-chief." He kicked a loose stone into the water. "Have things bottomed out at Arant and Devries?"

"We're all on one floor, now that so many attorneys have jumped ship." Sarah shrugged. "In some ways things are much better. St. John is taking it well. He says that the firm is back to where it was in his father's time."

"And Charlotte?"

"If you can believe your eyes, she's the devoted wife. The truth is anybody's guess."

They stood aside to let a pair of joggers pass.

"I often think about Sterling," Sarah said.

"Me, too."

"How did he become so unhinged? I thought of him as weak. But never evil."

"Evil?" Fallon shook his head. "But that weakness was fatal. When things went sour, he had no reserves, no resilience. He couldn't handle his divorce, his debts, being Wolfson's toady. Life was supposed to move onward and upward. When it didn't, he panicked."

"But murder? Was that weakness?"

"Don't you think so? The idea of facing his mistakes, of re-building his life, never seems to have occurred to him. He just struck out like a terrified child."

Sarah glanced at Fallon, whose eyes were fixed on the path before him. Was he thinking of his own struggles with alcohol and divorce? For a few minutes, they walked on in silence.

"Why do you think Deauville approached Sterling?" Sarah asked finally. "Why not proposition Wolfson directly?"

Fallon looked relieved to have the subject changed. "Put yourself in Deauville's place. Would you choose Felix Wolfson as a partner in crime? Or would you pick someone you could manipulate?"

"So Deauville cut a deal with Sterling. And Sterling was actually in touch with Maurice Politz before Deauville even showed up at the firm?"

Fallon nodded. "While we were all worrying about Irene Shaughnessy, Sterling already knew all about Oak Knoll. It was his job to make sure I got the information at the last possible minute so that there would be no opportunity for awkward questions."

"I always used to wonder why he seemed so confident about Irene Shaughnessy," Sarah mused.

"He almost managed to give the show away," Fallon agreed. "Unfortunately, none of us had any reason to suspect Politz's report."

"Except for Heidi," said Sarah. "She was always skeptical about the whole scenario."

"That's true," said Fallon. "She always saw too much."

They were silent again, thinking of Heidi.

Then Fallon smiled. "Much as I enjoy seeing you again, I actually called you with a very definite proposal. It involves my new office."